100首诗歌中英互译研究

张琼 著

Lakeside Poetic Bridge

100 Poems Translated Between Chinese and English

图书在版编目(CIP)数据

湖畔诗桥:100首诗歌中英互译研究=Lakeside Poetic Bridge 100 Poems Translated Between Chinese and English/张琼著.—武汉:武汉大学出版社,2020.12(2022.4重印)
ISBN 978-7-307-21650-1

Ⅰ.湖… Ⅱ.张… Ⅲ.诗歌—文学翻译—研究 Ⅳ.I106.2

中国版本图书馆 CIP 数据核字(2020)第 129380 号

责任编辑:李晶晶　　责任校对:李孟潇　　版式设计:韩闻锦

出版发行:**武汉大学出版社**　(430072　武昌　珞珈山)
（电子邮箱:cbs22@whu.edu.cn　网址:www.wdp.com.cn）
印刷:武汉邮科印务有限公司
开本:720×1000　1/16　印张:18.25　字数:235 千字　插页:1
版次:2020 年 12 月第 1 版　　2022 年 4 月第 2 次印刷
ISBN 978-7-307-21650-1　　定价:52.00 元

版权所有,不得翻印;凡购买我社的图书,如有质量问题,请与当地图书销售部门联系调换。

爱诗，译诗，论诗
——张琼译诗"三部曲"序
吴伟雄

张琼君的译诗"三部曲"包括：《湖畔诗风——中国经典古诗词100首英译研究》(武汉大学出版社)、《湖畔诗意——中国当代诗歌100首英译研究》(芝加哥学术出版社)、《湖畔诗桥——100首诗歌中英互译研究》(武汉大学出版社)。这"三部曲"从古至今，从中到外，总结了她多年来爱诗、译诗和论诗的丰硕成果。可喜可贺！她嘱我为之写序。我虽然也说得上爱诗、译过诗和写过一些论诗的文字，但水平有限，成果甚微，仍是一名票友，所以曾数次婉拒。但感于张琼君一再有嘱，且近年来一直和她就诗学问题展开讨论交流，还和她共同在武汉大学出版社出版《中英诗歌鉴赏》，诚意实在难违，只好奉命为之。

与诗结缘三步走：爱诗，译诗，论诗。

张琼君是肇庆学院外国语学院副教授，翻译研究所副所长，翻译学科带头人；广东省肇庆市翻译协会会长，华诗会会员及汉英双语诗刊《诗殿堂》翻译部执行主编。

在大学阶段，她就喜欢诗歌，买过诗集赏读，在大学执教翻译时，曾到中山大学进修，买了诗歌著作学习和研读。爱诗、赏读、研读之余，其五年前曾就唐代诗人王维《鹿柴》一诗的英译写了两篇研究论文——《〈鹿柴〉六个英译本的语篇功能分析》和《〈鹿柴〉六个英译本的经验功能分析》——在高校学报发表。可见她的研读,并非浮光掠影,而是渐入深度。她说,真正"恋上诗歌"是2018年夏天从《译原》电子杂志和中诗网《英诗同题翻译》栏目上译诗开始的。

自两年前爱上诗歌起,她就真正走上了译诗之路。《译原》电子杂志大概每月征译两期,古体诗和现代诗交替进行;《英诗同题翻译》大概每月一期。从一发端,她就一发不可收拾,尽管工作很忙,仍几乎不缺席上述两个平台每期的译文征集活动!

其译诗,走的是"译旧似旧""译新似新"的路子,最大的特色是以诗译诗,行文简洁,而无诗行膨胀的感觉;另外,其所译诗歌意思清晰,语义连贯,意境明朗,语法脉络和逻辑思路清晰。在用韵方面,其逐渐掌握了规律,韵式也逐步运用自如。

她完成征集译文后,还在译文之后,写上"译后小记"(或"译论""译评"),总结思路和技巧。其每期征译用热情做,"用力"实践,在量的方面积累经验;译后则"用心"总结,在质的方面提高,如怎样翻译(how),为什么这样翻译(why)。英语谚语有云:The person who knows how will always have a job. But the person who knows why will be boss.(知其然者,任事;知其所以然者,任人)且把"任人"理解为翻译的主人,掌握翻译的主动权吧。果然,近两年,她又在国内外刊物上陆续发表了四篇诗歌翻译研究论文,如《诗歌翻译,连贯重构与诗意再现——以司各特的〈狩猎歌〉为例》。

她对诗歌翻译是研究,已经不囿于"译"了,而且还涉足歌曲译配。所谓"译配",就是不仅仅单纯翻译诗歌一样的歌词,还必须让译出的歌词戴着原曲旋律的"镣铐",配合得当,自然顺畅地唱出来、唱得好!她译配的作品,陆续在中诗网和海外的"英国文学"电子平台发表,备受好评。她还撰写研究歌曲译配的学术论文。此外,她还在《诗殿堂》等诗刊发表自己的原创诗作。

张琼君译诗"三部曲",是她与诗结缘——爱诗,译诗,论诗——

三步走的结果，对有意与诗结缘的朋友有一定的启发和帮助。这大概可以形象地喻为——

学诗者的入门小苑。

初学诗的年轻人，可能觉得诗歌很难。我曾在大学开设"英语诗歌选读"课，有的学生心生疑问，"诗歌是不是很难呀？"其实，写诗，译诗，当然很难；但是，选读英语诗歌，而不是写和译啊！初学，可以选短小的诗歌学习。张琼君的译诗"三部曲"涉及古今中外的300首诗词，如果将其比作琳琅满目的自助餐，可以一道道地品尝，又可以根据喜好选尝，开卷一读，积少成多，终有收益。现在一些住宅，一进门就是"入户花园"，这"三部曲"，就起到学诗者的入门小苑的作用了。

译诗者的交流平台。

诗无达诂，译无定译。译者如何理解，译文就如何写成。以宋代诗人陈与义的诗《拒霜》的英译为例，可作说明。诗曰：

　　拒霜花已吐，吾宇不凄凉。天地虽肃杀，草木有芬芳。道人宴坐处，侍女古时妆。浓露湿丹脸，西风吹绿裳。

张琼君在"译后小记"上写道："诗题'拒霜'的英译是个难点，若单纯音译不能表达其义；若按字面直译为'the frost-proof blooms'，则不知为何种花卉；若用其学名似难出诗意诗境。笔者曾采用音译+意译的方法，译为'Jushuang, the Frost-Proof Blooms'。简洁一点，以'cotton rose'（木芙蓉）译之也未尝不可，诗文中写的就是拒霜不畏严寒，只是丢失"拒霜"这一中文花名，加大了读者的理解难度。诗无达诂，翻译总是得失之间的选择。"

这一期所有应征译文发表后，她把全部译文进行了研究梳理，不仅分析各译家对诗题的不同翻译，还分析了个人对"天地""草木"的不同理解，"道人""侍女"的意象差异，"侍女"与"拒霜"的关系，等等。

读者在选读其"三部曲"个别诗及其译文的时候，可以根据自己的理解，得出不同的结果(译文)，这实际上是和译者进行译诗的交流。

论诗者的思路发端。

张琼君译诗"三部曲"后面的"译后小记"是一大独特特点。这是译者理解思路，技巧说明或译诗理论的小结。"译后小记"是写诗歌翻译研究论文的发端。西南大学文旭教授说，翻译及翻译学研究最好的办法就是把规定、描写、解释融为一体，把 what，why，how 这三个问题结合起来，张琼君的诗歌翻译研究正是走的这一路线。所以，她近两年能在海内外期刊连续发表四篇诗歌翻译研究论文。

对此，本人亦颇有体会和实践。我有一位从事医疗工作的高中学友，其在申报副高级职称时，写了论文《手术治疗子宫脱垂的体会》，请我把论文摘要译为英语。我的译文，得到其校(现广州医科大学)教授的赞许，说"译得比学校年轻的英语教师好"。我就思考，"好在什么地方呢?"我总结出：除去枝叶，抓住主干；通盘考虑，信达求雅；不必形似，但求神似；专有名词，名从主人。这是我第一次写的"译后小记"，后来扩展成文——《理解理顺原文，译文才有条理——英译一篇妇产科医学论文摘要的体会》。此文在《中国科技翻译》1995 年第 3 期发表(知网可查)。后来，这位学友申报正高级职称写的论文，也让我英译其论文摘要。我还曾应中国海洋大学硕士生导师兼外事处首席翻译邹卫宁之约，为该校英译校训"海纳百川，取则行远"。邹老师客气地回函说："I think your translation of the 'mission statement' of our university is quite 'faithful, expressive and elegant'." 就译文是怎样组织出来的这个问题，我写了"英译小记"，全文在《中国海洋大学报》上发表,还附上了我的简介。

"译后小记",作用不小!

以诗译诗,脱离不了押韵问题。张琼君从不大注意韵译到认真实践韵译,爱上韵译,最后"译旧似旧",好,实在是好(It's not just good, but wonderful)!韵译产生"音美"。然而,"意美"是硬道理!韵译诗歌,必须警惕"以韵害意"。我愿和张琼君以及坚持"译旧似旧"的同好们共勉!诗歌是视觉的艺术,也是听觉的艺术,是时间的艺术,也是空间的艺术。写诗,译诗,诗歌翻译与研究需要时间的沉淀,不断地进取,希望张琼君坚持对诗歌及诗歌翻译的酷爱,加强诗学研究,在诗歌翻译与研究上继续新的探索。

我诚意地向诗歌翻译爱好者推荐张琼君的译诗"三部曲"。先睹为快(The sooner to read, the happier in deed)!

(吴伟雄,中国翻译协会第四届和五届理事,资深翻译家;长期从事地方外事单位管理和翻译工作,2006—2017年任北京理工大学珠海学院外国语学院教授。)

前　言

当詹姆斯·鲍斯韦尔问塞缪尔·约翰逊"什么是诗歌"时，约翰逊这样回答："先生，说什么不是诗歌要容易得多。我们都知道什么是光，但不容易说清楚光是什么。"为了便于理解，我们不妨再看看下面这两首诗，以及笔者拙译。

1. What Is Poetry?
By Eleanor Farjeon

What is Poetry? Who knows?
Not a rose, but the scent of the rose;
Not the sky, but the light in the sky;
Not the fly, but the gleam of the fly;
Not the sea, but the sound of the sea;
Not myself, but what makes me
See, hear, and feel something that prose
Cannot: and what it is, who knows?

1. 何为诗
埃莉诺·法杰恩

何为诗，孰知之乎？
非玫瑰，乃其香也，

非天空，乃其光也，
非萤虫，乃其亮也，
非大海，乃其声也。
非吾身，乃触吾心，
感吾耳目，而散文之不能也，
何为诗，孰知之乎？

2. Ars Poetica

By Archibald Macleish

A poem should be palpable and mute
As a globed fruit,

Dumb
As old medallions to the thumb,

Silent as the sleeve-worn stone
Of casement ledges where the moss has grown—

A poem should be wordless
As the flight of birds.

*

A poem should be motionless in time
As the moon climbs,

Leaving, as the moon releases
Twig by twig the night-entangled trees,

Leaving, as the moon behind the winter leaves,
Memory by memory the mind—

A poem should be motionless in time
As the moon climbs.

     *

A poem should be equal to:
Not true.

For all the history of grief
An empty doorway and a maple leaf.

For love
The leaning grasses and two lights above the sea—

A poem should not mean
But be.

2. 诗艺

阿奇博尔德·麦克利什

诗应静默而可感知
如滚圆果子

不语
如旧奖章之于拇指

不言如衣袖磨平
的窗台石，青苔悄生——

无声
如鸟翱翔

    *

诗应静驻时光
任月攀升

隽永，任月一枝一枝
解开被黑夜纠缠的树

隽永，任月在冬身后离去
记忆于心田——

诗应静驻时光
任月攀升

    *

诗不应
写实

人生寂寥
化作空阶枫叶飘

爱意缠绵
化作芳草依依光数点——

诗者，不言
而是也

笔者喜爱诗歌，偶尔兴起，也会写几行，真正译诗却还有个缘起。戊戌年仲夏，吴伟雄教授给我发来一首诗，我们探讨了一下翻译。过两日，问我还要修改吗，这才得知，吴教授在《译原》电子杂志翻译诗歌，邀我参与。就这样，从事多年翻译教学的我开始尝试诗歌翻译。翁显良教授曾说："外国文学作品的汉译，其成败关键，在于得作者之志，用汉语之长，求近似的效果。"如何才能得作者之志呢，我有幸跟随王东风教授学习语篇翻译，语篇的连贯分析、情景再现有助于理解原诗。遇到诗歌的格律韵式不懂，我就请教吴教授或求助于书本。随着时间的推移，我的译诗也散见于中诗网和《译原》《翻译中国》《暮雪诗刊》《长江诗歌》《中国诗影响》《诗殿堂》《肇庆学院学报》等报纸杂志。于是，我整理了自己翻译的部分诗歌，并撰写译论，集结成这个小册子，以求教于方家。

鲁迅先生曾提出关于中国文学创作的"三美"理论："意美以感心，一也；音美以感耳，二也；形美以感目，三也。"翻译家许渊冲先生，就将鲁迅的"三美"论移植到诗歌翻译，从而形成基于其本身翻译诗歌实践的"三美"论。在许渊冲先生看来，在翻译诗歌过程中，追求"真"和"美"并不冲突，追求美在一定程度上也保存了原诗的真，诗歌追求美，翻译追求真。诗无达诂，译无定法。诗歌翻译是有遗憾的艺术，正如屠岸先生所说，不论译者怎样忠实于原作，译作和原作之间总会存在距离，百分之百原汁原味的诗歌翻译是不存在的。据说美国诗人弗罗斯特曾说："Poetry is what gets lost in translation。"（诗意乃翻译中失去的东西）这意味着诗歌翻译难以完美。

诗歌翻译，笔者尽量以格律诗译格律诗，以自由诗译自由诗，诗歌的音韵节奏，有时甚至标点符号，尽量与原诗一致，尽力传递所译诗歌的原貌。我追求译诗意义不背原诗，语义清晰，行文流畅，有画面感，自然去雕饰，尽量少用注。诗歌翻译我们一直在路上，尽力在"求真""求美"之间找一个最佳平衡点。以下略述二三例。

以诗译诗，译旧如旧。《春日》是宋代思想家、教育家朱熹创作的一首诗。此诗表面上看是一首写景诗，描绘了春日美好的景致；实际上是一首哲理诗，表达了诗人于乱世中追求圣人之道的美好愿望。全诗寓理趣于形象之中，构思运笔堪称奇妙。在翻译这首诗时，我们采用五音步抑扬格为主旋律，押韵格式为aabb。原诗与译诗如下：

3. 春日
〔宋〕朱熹

胜日寻芳泗水滨，
无边光景一时新。
等闲识得东风面，
万紫千红总是春。

3. Spring Day
By Zhu Xi

I'm seeking scenes by Si River on a sunny day：
Grass lush, flowers blooming, a thriving way.
Refreshed by a sudden breath of spring in air，
I see in myriads of colors spring hide there.

译新如新，保留原诗的意象，行文流畅。如海子的《九月》，这首诗歌极其沉痛，充满神秘氛围，渺远的时间与旷阔的空间扭结纠缠在一起，生命与死亡在互相诠释，翻译就是体验和再现诗人所感所想。诗人借助"草原""野花""秋风""马头琴""明月"等意象，营造旷远深邃的悲秋寂寥，故将"九月"译为"Lunar September"，因为农历的九月有更多的文化遐想。翻译时坚持"译意不译字"，如"我的琴声呜咽"，译为"My strings sob"(我的琴在呜咽);"泪水全无",不译"without tears",而译为"with tearless grief"(欲哭无泪的悲伤)。原诗和拙译如下:

4. 九月

海子

目击众神死亡的草原上野花一片
远在远方的风比远方更远
我的琴声呜咽 泪水全无
我把这远方的远归还草原
一个叫马头 一个叫马尾
我的琴声呜咽 泪水全无

远方只有在死亡中凝聚野花一片
明月如镜高悬草原映照千年岁月
我的琴声呜咽 泪水全无
只身打马过草原

4. Lunar September

By Haizi

The prairie witnessed the death of pantheon presents boundless wild flowers
The wind afar is even farther away from afar
My strings sob with tearless grief
I return to the prairie the afar from afar
One is called horse-head, the other horse-tail

My strings sob with tearless grief

The afar only in death converges a sheet of wild flowers

The mirror-like moon hangs high over the land reflecting time of thousands of years

My strings sob with tearless grief

Alone I ride a horse across the prairie

诗歌节奏如同呼吸，非常重要，下面举一例说明再现原诗节奏。美国诗人艾米莉·狄金森的诗歌主要写生活情趣、自然、生命等，诗风凝练、比喻新颖、喜用格律、不顾语法，极富独创性。她的 *A Bird Came down the Walk* 是一首白描诗，诗人偶遇一只小鸟吃虫，主角是小鸟，"我"是旁观者。狄金森用简洁的笔触勾勒出小鸟的形象，用小鸟怡然自得捕食蚯蚓、饮水、让路等一连串的动作(came down, bit, ate, drank, hopped, glanced, stirred, unrolled, rowed)去塑造自己，而作者却隐蔽起来(I saw, I thought)，后来因"我"的介入(I offered)，惊扰了小鸟的安宁，结果小鸟展翅飞走。全诗共分5个诗节，每节4行，只有一个句号，是一个完整连贯的动画。原诗以抑扬格三音步为主旋律(只有每节第三行是四音步)，拙译保留原诗格律和节奏，保留原诗标点符号，以顿代步，尽量再现原文的音韵节奏。

5. A Bird Came down the Walk

By Emily Dickinson

A Bird /came down /the Walk—
He did/ not know /I saw—
He bit/ an Ang/le Worm/ in halves
And ate /the fel/low, raw,

And then/ he drank /a Dew

From a /conve/nient Grass—

And then/ hopped side/wise to /the Wall

To let/ a Bee/tle pass—

He glanced /with rap/id eyes

That hur/ried all /around—

They looked /like fright/ened Beads, /I thought—

He stirred/ his Vel/vet Head

Like one/ in danger, / Cautious,

I of/fered him/ a Crumb

And he/ unro/lled his /feathers

And rowed/ him sof/ter home—

Than Oars /divide /the Ocean,

Too sil/ver for /a seam—

Or But/terflies, /off Banks /of Noon

Leap, / plashless /as they swim.

5. 小鸟沿小径走来
[美]艾米莉·狄金森

小鸟/沿小径/走来——

不知/一旁/我在瞧——

他把/一条/蚯蚓/啄开

再吃掉/那家伙, /生嚼,

他将/清露/饮吞
取自/近旁/草叶上——
又侧身/跳到/旁边/墙脚根
来给/甲虫/把路让——

急促地/左顾/右盼
他那/滴溜溜的/眼眸——
活像/受惊的/珠子，/我想——
见他/抖了抖/天鹅绒的头

好像/身处险境，/十分小心，
我给他/分点/碎面包
而他/立刻/展开/羽翎
往回/飞去/一路轻飘——

胜过/船桨/划海面，
波光/银白/水无痕——
胜过/蝴蝶，/晌午 /草埂边
跃下，/游弋/无溅声。

《湖畔诗风——中国经典古诗词100首英译研究》《湖畔诗意——中国现代诗歌100首英译研究》《湖畔诗桥——100首诗歌中英互译研究》是一个诗歌翻译系列，古代诗歌追求诗风，现代诗歌追求诗意，中英诗歌互译谓之诗桥。本书《湖畔诗桥——100首诗歌中英互译研究》选取了汉语诗歌50首，英国、爱尔兰及美国诗人的诗歌50首进行中英互译研究。所选诗歌体裁不一，风格各异，有古代经典诗歌，也有现代优秀诗歌作品。笔者在翻译时尽量接近原诗风格，部分翻译诗歌在相关电子刊物和纸媒已经发表，编入本书时有所修正，并增加"译后小记"。本书适合大学英语专业和非英语专业学生、英语教师、诗歌爱好者和诗歌翻译人员阅读、参考。欢迎方家批评指正！

诗歌和诗歌的翻译，提高了我的感性素质和审美情趣，加深了我对生活的体验和认知，让我精神愉悦。译路走来，首先得感谢北京理工大学珠海学院外国语学院吴伟雄教授。我们经常一起探讨诗歌翻译，吴教授总是诲人不倦，给了我莫大的鼓舞。吴教授对诗歌的热忱，以及他经常提到的许渊冲先生对诗歌的热爱，无不激励着我。

特别感谢原复旦大学教师、现美国德宝大学语言研究中心主任，汉学教授，华诗会会长，汉英双语纸质诗刊《诗殿堂》总编徐英才先生。徐教授是我诗歌翻译路上的一位导师，他博学多才、治学严谨，关爱后生学子，并写了如下评语激励我。

> 汉语是一个多韵语，同韵字相当多，这为格律诗的创作创造了有利条件。而英语是一种少韵语，同韵字相当少，因此韵译中国古诗词的难度相当大，稍不留神，译文就会流于生硬、偏离，或者基本就是那几个多韵字捣来捣去。本书译者张琼勇于直面困难，坚持采用韵译法来韵译诗歌，她的译文对原文的表达意思到位，声音和谐，常有妙笔生花处，值得一读。对现代诗的翻译，张琼努力追求诗歌的意境再造和诗歌的内在联系。她现代诗的英译自然连贯，也值得一读。
>
> ——徐英才

特别感谢中山大学王东风教授，跟随他访学进修一年，让我受益匪浅。感谢国际学术期刊《翻译中国》的主编，上海大学赵彦春教授。在翻译中遇到问题，赵教授马上解答，并写成博文，给了我莫大鼓舞。

诗歌翻译路上，感谢《译原》电子杂志栏目主持人解斌，在其策划和主持下我进行了中国古诗词英译、中国现代诗歌英译，以及诗音画一诗多译等。感谢中诗网《双语诗界》栏目编辑王磊先生，该栏目为广大诗歌爱好者提供了诗歌交流学习平台。感谢《诗殿堂》主编，山东政法大学颜海峰副教授。感谢《诗殿堂》副主编石永浩先生、张俊峰先生。感谢王昌玲、铁冰等诗歌译友。大家一起探讨诗歌翻译，受益良多，在此，一并致谢。

张琼

2020 年 1 月于肇庆星湖湖畔

Preface

When James Boswell asked Samuel Johnson, "What is poetry?" Johnson answered: "Why, Sir, it is much easier to say what it is not. We all know what light is; but it is not easy to tell what it is." For a better understanding, Let's begin with reading two English poetry and my translation.

1. What Is Poetry?

By Eleanor Farjeon

What is Poetry? Who knows?
Not a rose, but the scent of the rose;
Not the sky, but the light in the sky;
Not the fly, but the gleam of the fly;
Not the sea, but the sound of the sea;
Not myself, but what makes me
See, hear, and feel something that prose
Cannot: and what it is, who knows?

1. 何为诗

埃莉诺·法杰恩

何为诗,孰知之乎?
非玫瑰,乃其香也,

非天空，乃其光也，
非萤虫，乃其亮也，
非大海，乃其声也。
非吾身，乃触吾心，
感吾耳目，而散文之不能也，
何为诗，孰知之乎？

2. Ars Poetica

By Archibald Macleish

A poem should be palpable and mute
As a globed fruit,

Dumb
As old medallions to the thumb,

Silent as the sleeve-worn stone
Of casement ledges where the moss has grown—

A poem should be wordless
As the flight of birds.

*

A poem should be motionless in time
As the moon climbs,

Leaving, as the moon releases
Twig by twig the night-entangled trees,

Leaving, as the moon behind the winter leaves,
Memory by memory the mind—

A poem should be motionless in time
As the moon climbs.
*
A poem should be equal to:
Not true.

For all the history of grief
An empty doorway and a maple leaf.

For love
The leaning grasses and two lights above the sea—

A poem should not mean
But be.

2. 诗艺
阿奇博尔德·麦克利什

诗应静默而可感知
如滚圆果子

不语
如旧奖章之于拇指

不言如衣袖磨平
的窗台石，青苔悄生——

无声
如鸟翱翔
   *
诗应静驻时光
任月攀升

隽永，任月一枝一枝
解开被黑夜纠缠的树

隽永，任月在冬身后离去
记忆于心田——

诗应静驻时光
任月攀升
   *
诗不应
写实

人生寂寥
化作空阶枫叶飘

爱意缠绵
化作芳草依依光数点——

诗者，不言
而是也

I loved poetry, occasionally I wrote a few lines, but the real translation of poetry had an origin. Two years ago, Professor Wu Weixiong sent me a poem and we discussed about the translation. Two days later, he asked me if I had any revision before I learned that Professor Wu had invited me to participate in translating poetry in an electronic magazine. In this way, I began to try poetry translation after years of teaching college student translation. As Professor Weng Xianliang once said: the key to the success or failure of translating foreign literary works is to gain the author's will, to use the Chinese language to achieve similar results. How can I get the author's ambition? I have followed Professor Wang Dongfeng to study of text translation, which is quite helpful. If I happen to have a question about the rhythm or rhyme of poetry, I'll discuss with Professor Wu. With the passage of time, my translated poems are published in newspapers and magazines such as China Poetry Website, *Translation of China* and *Poetry Hall*, *Journal of Zhaoqing University*, etc. Therefore, I select some of these poems with studies and assembled them into this anthology.

The great Chinese writer Mr. Lu Xun once put forward the theory of "three aesthetic principles" about Chinese literature creation: "Meaning for the heart, sound for the ear, form for the eye." (general meaning, my translation) Professor Xu Yuanchong transplanted Lu Xun's "three aesthetic principles" to poetry translation based on his own practice of translating poetry. In Mr. Xu Yuanchong's view, in the process of translating poetry, the pursuit of "truth" and "beauty" does not conflict, the pursuit of beauty also preserves the truth of the original poem to a certain extent. Poetry pursues beauty, and translation pursues truth. Poetry has no exegesis, and translation has no definite method. The translation of poetry is a regrettable art. As Mr. Tu'an said, no matter how faithful the translator is to the original, there is always a distance between the translation and the original, and a 100% authentic translation of poetry does not exist. It is said American poet Frost once said "poetry is what gets lost in translation", which means translation of poetry is always an imperfect art.

In the process of poetry translation, we try to follow the rhythm and rhyme of the original poetry besides the meaning, sometimes even punctuation, as far as possible consistent with the original poem. We pursue the exact meaning of the original poem, clear, fluent natural expression with few notes. We try to find a balance point in the continuum of "seeking truth" and "seeking beauty". Let's illustrate with two or three examples.

"Spring Day" is a poem written by Zhu Xi, a thinker and educator in the Song Dynasty. It seems that literally the poem is a simple landscape poem, depicting the beautiful scenery of spring; in fact, it is a philosophical poem, expressing the poet's good desire to pursue the way of the Saint Confucius in troubled times. The conception of the poem is full of images. In translating this classical Chinese poem, we adopt the iambic pentameter and follow the rhyme format aabb. The original and translated poems are as follows.

3. 春日

〔宋〕朱熹

胜日寻芳泗水滨，
无边光景一时新。
等闲识得东风面，
万紫千红总是春。

3. Spring Day
By Zhu Xi

I'm seeking scenes by Si River on a sunny day:
Grass lush, flowers blooming, a thriving way.
Refreshed by a sudden breath of spring in air,
I see in myriads of colors spring hide there.

The free verse in modern times is written in natural rhythm with abundant images, which cares little about rhyme. *Lunar September* written by Haizi is a typical free verse with a tone extremely painful, full of mysterious atmosphere, ethereal time and broad space kink entangled together, life and death in the interpretation of each other. In the translation of this poem, we try to experience and reproduce the poet's feelings. With the images of "prairie" "wild flowers" "wind" "horse-head qin" "moon", the poet creates a melancholy autumn. In the translation, we focus on the poeticity besides the meaning. The original poem and translation are as follows.

4. 九月
海子

目击众神死亡的草原上野花一片
远在远方的风比远方更远
我的琴声呜咽 泪水全无
我把这远方的远归还草原
一个叫马头 一个叫马尾

我的琴声呜咽 泪水全无

远方只有在死亡中凝聚野花一片
明月如镜高悬草原映照千年岁月
我的琴声呜咽 泪水全无
只身打马过草原

4. Lunar September

By Haizi

The prairie witnessed the death of pantheon presents boundless wild flowers

The wind afar is even farther away from afar

My strings sob with tearless grief

I return to the prairie the afar from afar

One is called horse-head, the other horse-tail

My strings sob with tearless grief

The afar only in death converges a sheet of wild flowers

The mirror-like moon hangs high over the land reflecting time of thousands of years

My strings sob with tearless grief

Alone I ride a horse across the prairie

Rhythm is the breath of a poetry, here is another example below. "*A Bird Came down the Walk*" is iambic trimeter poem with some variation. The whole poem is divided into 5 verses, 4 lines each, with only one full stop, which is a complete and coherent animation. Dickinson sketched the image of "bird" with concise strokes in a series of movements (came down, bit, ate, drank, hopped, glanced, stirred, unrolled, rowed), while she hid herself in the background (e. g. I saw, I thought). Later, "my" intervention (e. g. I offered) disturbed the peace of the bird. As a result, the bird spread its wings and flew away. "Dun" is a pause according to the meaning group in Chinese poetry, which is not equivalent to foot in English poetry, but can be used to express the rhythm of the English poetry in a certain extend in E-C poetry translation. In the translation of this poem, we adopt "Dun" to create the same effect of the original rhythm and follow the same punctuation to reproduce the rhythm of whole poetic picture. The rhythm analysis of the original poem and my translation are as follows.

5. A Bird Came down the Walk
By Emily Dickinson

A Bird /came down /the Walk—
He did/ not know /I saw—
He bit/ an Ang/le Worm/ in halves
And ate /the fel/low, raw,

And then/ he drank /a Dew
From a /conve/nient Grass—
And then/ hopped side/wise to /the Wall
To let/ a Bee/tle pass—

He glanced /with rap/id eyes
That hur/ried all /around—
They looked /like fright/ened Beads, /I thought—

He stirred/ his Vel/vet Head

Like one/ in danger, / Cautious,
I of/fered him/ a Crumb
And he/ unro/lled his /feathers
And rowed/ him sof/ter home—

Than Oars /divide /the Ocean,
Too sil/ver for /a seam—
Or But/terflies, /off Banks /of Noon
Leap, / plashless /as they swim.

5. 小鸟沿小径走来

[美]艾米莉·狄金森

小鸟/沿小径/走来——
不知/一旁/我在瞧——
他把/一条/蚯蚓/啄开
再吃掉/那家伙,/生嚼,

他将/清露/饮吞
取自/近旁/草叶上——
又侧身/跳到/旁边/墙脚根
来给/甲虫/把路让——

急促地/左顾/右盼
他那/滴溜溜的/眼眸——
活像/受惊的/珠子,/我想——

见他/抖了抖/毛茸茸的头

好像/身处险境,/十分小心,
我给他/分点/碎面包
而他/立刻/展开/羽翎
往回/飞去/一路轻飘——

胜过/船桨/划海面,
波光/银白/水无痕——
胜过/蝴蝶,/晌午/草埂边
跃下,/游弋/无溅声。

Lakeside Poetic Breeze: *English Translation of 100 Classic Chinese Poems*, *Lakeside Poetic Sense*: *English Translation of 100 Contemporary Chinese Poems*, and *Lakeside Poetic Bridge*: *100 Poems Translated Between Chinese and English* are a series of poetry translation studies. In this book, 100 classic Chinese poems before the Qing Dynasty are selected and arranged according to the order of the dynasty. Some of the translated poems have been published in the electronic journals and print media and revised in this book. This book is suitable for college English majors and non-English majors, English teachers, poetry lovers and poetry translators.

Poetry and poetry translation have improved my perceptual quality and aesthetic taste, enriched my life experience and cognition, and made me spiritually happy. In this poetry translation way, I appreciate all those who have cared, helped and inspired me. First of all, I would like to thank Professor Wu Weixiong from Zhuhai Institute of Technology, Beijing Institute of Technology. We often discuss poetry translation together, and

Professor Wu has given me great encouragement. Professor Wu's enthusiasm for poetry as well as his often mention of Mr. Xu Yuanchong's love of poetry, all inspired me.

I would like to express my warmest thanks to Mr. Xu Yingcai, former Fudan University teacher, Professor of Sinology in the Language Department of Depaul University, President of the Chinese Poetry Society, and Editor-in-chief of the Chinese-English bilingual journal *Poetry Hall*. Professor Xu is a good teacher on my way of poetry translation. He is knowledgeable, rigorous and caring. He writes the following comments to inspire me:

> Chinese is a rhyme-rich language with a broad spectrum of shared syllables, which facilitates an easy writing of rhyming poetry, while English is a rhyme-poor language with quite limited number of similar syllables, which creates a great difficulty for rhyme-translating traditional Chinese poetry. Therefore, rhyme-translating traditional Chinese poems tends to be effortful in wording, disloyal to the original, and repeated use of the very few rhyming friendly syllables. However, in translating this anthology of classical Chinese poems, Zhang Qiong confronts the difficulty and insists in rhyme translating. Her translation conveys the meaning of the original with harmonious rhymes and rhythms, and often blossoms. Her translation is a rewarding reading. In the translation of modern poetry, Zhang Qiong makes every effort to recreate the poetic imagery and inner coherence. Her translation is natural and coherent, which is worth reading too.
>
> ——Xu Yingcai

I would also like to thank Professor Wang Dongfeng of Sun Yat-sen University for a year's translation study guided by him. Thanks go to Professor Zhao Yanchun, Editor-in-Chief of the International Academic Journal *Translating China*. When I had a question about poetry translation, Professor Zhao immediately answered and wrote a blog, which gave me great encouragement. I would also give thanks to Mr. Xie Bin, column host of *Yiyuan Electronic Magazine*, Mr. Wang Lei, column host of *Translation of Chinese Poetry to Foreign Versions* and *Translation of Foreign Poetry to Chinese Version* in China Poetry Website. Thanks also go to my editorial colleagues Mr. Yan Haifeng, associate professor of Shandong University of Political Science and Law; Mr. Shi Yonghao, associate professor of Shandong University of Political Science and Law; Mr. Zhang Junfeng, English teacher of USST; my peer poetry translator Ms. Wang Changling and Mr. Iceiron. We have been discussing the translation of poetry together, which benefits me a lot.

Zhang Qiong

Jan. 2020 by Star Lake, Zhaoqing

目 录/Content

第一部分　汉语诗歌英译
Part I　Chinese-English Poetry Translation

1. 我们 ·· 003
   We ·· 003
2. 解脱 ·· 005
   Relief ·· 005
3. 秋江的晚上 ·· 007
   Autumn Dusk on the River ·· 007
4. 偶然 ·· 009
   An Encounter ··· 009
5. 沙扬娜拉 ··· 011
   ——赠日本女郎 ··· 011
   Farewell ··· 011
   　—To a Japanese Lady ··· 011
6. 季候 ·· 013
   Season ·· 013
7. 消息 ·· 015
   The Message ··· 015

8. 教我如何不想她 ·· 017
   How Can I Not Miss Her There ···················· 018
9. 窗外 ·· 020
   Outside the Window ··································· 020
10. 小诗 ··· 022
    A Little Poem ·· 022
11. 不足之感 ·· 024
    Insufficiency ··· 024
12. 光明 ··· 026
    Light ·· 026
13. 秋晨 ··· 029
    Autumn Morning ······································· 029
14. 再生 ··· 031
    Rebirth ··· 031
15. 早寒 ··· 033
    Early Chill ·· 033
16. 断章 ··· 035
    Fragment ·· 035
17. 你是人间的四月天 ·· 037
    You Are the April Day in the World ·············· 038
18. 时间 ··· 040
    Time ·· 040
19. 无题 ··· 042
    Untitled ·· 042
20. 情愿 ··· 044
    I Would Rather ·· 045

21. 八月的忧愁 ······ 047
    August Blues ······ 047

22. 笑 ······ 049
    Smiles ······ 049

23. 深夜里听到乐声 ······ 051
    The Music I Hear Late at Night ······ 052

24. 仍然 ······ 054
    As Usual ······ 054

25. 山中一个夏夜 ······ 056
    A Summer Night in the Mountains ······ 057

26. 记忆 ······ 059
    Memory ······ 059

27. 题剔空菩提叶 ······ 061
    Ode to a Hollow Bodi Leaf ······ 061

28. 静坐 ······ 063
    Meditation ······ 063

29. 那一晚 ······ 065
    That Night ······ 066

30. 一首桃花 ······ 068
    Ode to Peach Blossoms ······ 068

31. 诗的葬礼 ······ 070
    Funeral of a Poem ······ 070

32. 笑的种子 ······ 072
    The Seed of Laughter ······ 072

33. 雨景 ······ 074
    The Scenes of Rain ······ 074

34. 雨巷 ·· 076
    An Alley in the Rain ··· 077
35. 蛇 ·· 080
    Snake ··· 080
36. 我是一条小河 ·· 082
    I Am a River ·· 083
37. 我们有时度过一个亲密的夜 ·· 085
    Sometimes We Spend an Intimate Night ··························· 085
38. 我爱这土地 ··· 087
    I Love This Land ··· 087
39. 一朵野花 ·· 089
    A Wild Flower ·· 089
40. 冬夜 ·· 091
    A Winter Night ··· 091
41. 云 ·· 093
    Clouds ·· 093
42. 远和近 ··· 095
    Distant and Close ·· 095
43. 微微的希望 ··· 097
    A Glimmer of Hope ·· 097
44. 门前 ·· 099
    On the Doorstep ··· 100
45. 错误 ·· 103
    A Mistake ··· 103
46. 她那颗小小的心 ··· 105
    Her Little Heart ··· 105

47. 从前慢 ········· 107
   Old Days Slow ········· 107
48. 秋 ········· 109
   Autumn ········· 109
49. 面朝大海，春暖花开 ········· 110
   A Promising Life ········· 110
50. 九月 ········· 113
   Lunar September ········· 113

第二部分　英语诗歌汉译

Part II　English-Chinese Poetry Translation

51. *Since Brass, Nor Stone, Nor Earth,*
Nor Boundless Sea ········· 117
   金铜、岩石、大地或海洋 ········· 117
52. *When, in Disgrace with Fortune and*
Men's Eyes ········· 119
   时运不济遭贬谤 ········· 119
53. *Farewell Sweet Grove* ········· 122
   再见，美丽树林 ········· 122
54. *To Celia* ········· 124
   致西莉亚 ········· 124
55. *To Blossoms* ········· 126
   花儿 ········· 127
56. *To a Young Lady* ········· 129
   致佳人 ········· 129

- 57. *Eternity* ··· 131
  - 永恒 ··· 131
- 58. *The Reverie of Poor Susan* ··· 133
  - 苏珊幻梦 ··· 134
- 59. *The Lost Love* ·· 136
  - 失落的爱 ··· 136
- 60. *Lines Written in Early Spring* ·· 138
  - 早春随笔 ··· 139
- 61. *The Daffodils* ·· 141
  - 水仙花 ·· 142
- 62. *Desideria* ··· 145
  - 渴慕怀旧 ··· 145
- 63. *My Heart Leaps up When I Behold* ···································· 148
  - 凝眸，我心雀跃 ··· 148
- 64. *Hunting Song* ··· 150
  - 狩猎歌 ·· 151
- 65. *Love's Philosophy* ·· 155
  - 爱的哲学 ··· 155
- 66. *The Owl and the Pussy Cat* ·· 157
  - 猫头鹰和小猫咪 ··· 158
- 67. *The Night Has a Thousand Eyes* ······································· 161
  - 黑夜有一千只眼睛 ·· 161
- 68. *On the Sale by Auction of Keats' Love Letters* ···················· 163
  - 济慈情书被拍卖有感 ··· 163
- 69. *On the Hill-Side* ·· 166
  - 山坡上 ·· 166

70. *Leisure* ·· 168
　　闲暇 ··· 169

71. *Remember Me When I Am Gone Away* ············ 171
　　请勿忘我，当我离开 ································· 171

72. *What Is Poetry?* ·· 173
　　何为诗 ·· 173

73. *When You Are Old* ···································· 175
　　当你老了 ··· 175

74. *A Dream Within a Dream* ··························· 178
　　梦中之梦 ··· 179

75. *I Hear America Singing* ····························· 181
　　我听见美利坚在歌唱 ································· 182

76. *A Bird Came down the Walk* ······················ 184
　　小鸟沿小径走来 ······································· 185

77. *From Blank to Blank* ································ 187
　　来自虚无　去往虚无 ································· 187

78. *I Died for Beauty* ····································· 189
　　我为美而死 ··· 189

79. *I'm Nobody! Who Are You?* ························ 191
　　我是无名小辈，你呢? ······························· 191

80. *The Soul Selects Her Own Society* ·············· 193
　　灵魂选择自己的伴侣 ································· 193

81. *I Took One Draught of Life* ······················· 195
　　我啜饮过生命的琼浆 ································· 195

82. *Wild Nights* ·· 197
　　狂夜 ··· 197

- 83. *Sand Dunes* ……………………………………………………… 199
  - 沙丘 ……………………………………………………………… 200
- 84. *The Pasture* ……………………………………………………… 202
  - 牧场 ……………………………………………………………… 202
- 85. *Stopping by Woods on a Snowy Evening* ……………………… 204
  - 雪夜林边小驻 …………………………………………………… 205
- 86. *Acquainted with the Night* ……………………………………… 207
  - 熟谙黑夜 ………………………………………………………… 207
- 87. *Dust of Snow* …………………………………………………… 210
  - 雪尘 ……………………………………………………………… 210
- 88. *Fragmentary Blue* ……………………………………………… 212
  - 蓝色碎片 ………………………………………………………… 212
- 89. *Fire and Ice* ……………………………………………………… 214
  - 火与冰 …………………………………………………………… 214
- 90. *The Road Not Taken* …………………………………………… 216
  - 未选择之路 ……………………………………………………… 217
- 91. *Fog* ………………………………………………………………… 219
  - 雾 ………………………………………………………………… 219
- 92. *The Red Wheelbarrow* ………………………………………… 221
  - 红色手推车 ……………………………………………………… 221
- 93. *Ars Poetica* ……………………………………………………… 223
  - 诗艺 ……………………………………………………………… 224
- 94. *Dreams* …………………………………………………………… 228
  - 梦想 ……………………………………………………………… 228
- 95. *Do Not Stand at My Grave and Weep* ………………………… 230
  - 不要悲伤我墓前 ………………………………………………… 230

96. *Oil That Glitters* ………………………………… 232
   闪光的石油 …………………………………………… 232
97. *Parting* ……………………………………………… 234
   分别 …………………………………………………… 235
98. *A Farewell* ………………………………………… 237
   告别 …………………………………………………… 237
99. *My Heart's in the Highlands* …………………… 239
   我心在苏格兰高地 …………………………………… 240
100. *We Real Cool* …………………………………… 242
    我们真酷 ……………………………………………… 242

参考文献 …………………………………………………… 244

第一部分
汉语诗歌英译

Part I
Chinese-English
Poetry Translation

1. 我们

宗白华

我们并立天河下。

人间已落沉睡里。

天上的双星

映在我们的两心里。

我们握着手，看着天，不语。

一个神秘的微颤

经过我们两心深处。

1. *We*

By Zong Baihua

We stand side by side under the Milky Way.

The world has fallen into a deep sleep.

Altair and Vega

Are reflected in our hearts.

Hand in hand, we look up into the sky, silent.

A mysterious ripple

Riffles through the depths of our hearts.

译后小记

《我们》是现代诗人宗白华(1897—1986)创作的一首新诗,是一首相当别致的情诗。诗歌描绘了男女主人公于七夕夜半幽会在"天河下",人间万籁俱寂,天上的双星正在"鹊桥相会",这又引发了主人公的思考,本来甜蜜幸福的心理转变成了苦涩和担忧。结尾两句意味深长,主人公从自然景象中妙悟到了人生命运,对情感进行了哲理上的升华。在诗里,客观景物已经成为诗人主观情思的象征。这"情思"的产生虽为"双星"所触发,但却融入了诗人悲剧性的爱情体验。全诗语言精炼含蓄,精美典雅,抒情恬淡自然,耐人寻味。

诗中"天河""双星"源于神话故事《牛郎和织女》,译文分别用"the Milky Way"和"Altair and Vega"译出。希腊神话与中国神话,两者的文化意象并不相同,但都可营造一种神秘气氛,达到相同的认知效果。诗中的"我们",有时是主语"we",有时是定语"our"。"一个神秘的微颤/经过我们两心深处",译者将原诗的"微颤"转化为具体意象,译为"A mysterious ripple / Riffles through the depths of our hearts"(一股神秘的涟漪穿过我们的心灵深处)。

2. 解脱

宗白华

心中一段最后的幽凉
几时才能解脱呢?
银河的月,照我楼上。
笛声远远传来——
月的幽凉
心的幽凉
同化入宇宙的幽凉了。

2. *Relief*

By Zong Baihua

The last chilly cool of my heart,

When will it be set free?

The moonlight from the galaxy floods on my loft.

A melody of the flute comes from afar—

The chilly cool of the moon,

The chilly cool of my heart,

All melt into the chilly cool cosmos.

译后小记

首句,似乎作者等待解脱已经多时,尾句,远处笛声悠悠而至,月的幽凉、心的幽凉同化入宇宙的幽凉了,作者瞬间得以解脱,前后呼应。

这首诗歌比较抽象,重意境,"幽凉"一词不好懂。紧扣题目"解脱",诗人想要从"幽凉"里解脱,根据语篇的连贯性来理解作者情感态度的一致性,作者之心境应是接近"心灰意冷""清冷""凄凉",而非"凉爽",故"幽凉"一词以"chilly cool"译之。

拙译注重意境的营造,第二句,"银河的月,照我楼上。"照"译为"flood",意思是"银河的月如流水一般,静静地泻在这阁楼之上"。第三句"笛声远远传来——","传"译为"come",意思是"悠扬的笛声飘然而至"。第四句占三行,读来心理节奏加快,仿佛等待已久的解脱,在笛声悠扬而至的瞬间发生。译诗力求意境和节奏与原诗一致。

3. 秋江的晚上

刘大白

归巢的鸟儿，

尽管是倦了，

还驮着斜阳回去。

双翅一翻，

把斜阳掉在江上；

头白的芦苇，

也妆成一瞬的红颜了。

3. Autumn Dusk on the River

By Liu Dabai

A homing bird,

Tired though,

Carries on its back the setting sun.

Flapping its wings,

It has dropped the setting sun into the river;

The white-headed reeds

Blush in a rush.

译后小记

《秋江的晚上》是中国新诗运动主要倡导者之一——刘大白(1880—1932)先生的名诗,描写日落大江的空灵与梦幻,动静相宜,画面感很强。一诗两节,每节是完整的一句话。第一节的"鸟儿……驮……"用了拟人手法;第二节的"斜阳掉在江上",以及"白头芦苇,妆成红颜"可谓夸张的比拟手法,全诗短小,然意味深长。

译诗保持原诗结构,仍用两节,每节以完整一句译之。译诗中归巢之鸟如同归家之人,第一节用了"A homing bird tired…carried…"。第二节保留拟人修辞,前后承接连贯,仿佛"斜阳掉入江中的瞬间,白头芦苇羞红了脸"。为生动呈现画面,译诗采用一般现在时。

4. 偶然

徐志摩

我是天空里的一片云,
偶尔投影在你的波心——
你不必讶异,
更无须欢喜——
在转瞬间消灭了踪影。

你我相逢在黑夜的海上,
你有你的,我有我的,方向;
你记得也好,
最好你忘掉,
在这交会时互放的光亮!

4. *An Encounter*

By Xu Zhimo

I'm a cloud in the sky

By chance casting a shadow on the ripples of your mind—

You don't have to be surprised;

There is no need to rejoice—

I'll disappear in a blink of an eye.

I run into you in the sea of night,

You have your direction, I have mine;

You may remember,

But you'd better forget

The casual spark to each other at the first sight!

译后小记

《偶然》是现代诗人徐志摩于1926年5月创作的一首诗。此诗主要是诗人对人生、情感的深切感悟，诗人于其中表达了对爱与美的消逝的感叹，也透露出对这些美好情愫的眷顾之情。全诗两段十行，上下节格律对称，珠圆玉润，朗朗上口，余味无穷，意溢于言外。

译诗注意"偶然"一词的处理：诗题"偶然"用名词"encounter"（邂逅，不期而遇）译出；第一节的"偶尔"不译为副词"occasionally"，而译为"by chance"（碰巧）；第二节"在这交会时互放的光亮"也是偶然的，加一词"casual"（偶然的）。译诗采用自然流畅的表达，行尾押韵。

5. 沙扬娜拉

——赠日本女郎

徐志摩

最是那一低头的温柔,
像一朵水莲花不胜凉风的娇羞,
道一声珍重,道一声珍重,
那一声珍重里有蜜甜的忧愁——
沙扬娜拉!

5. Farewell

—To a Japanese Lady

By Xu Zhimo

Especially tender is thy bowing head,
Shy as a waterlily caressed by the cool breeze.
Fare thee well, fare thee well!
Thine sweet voice sounds sentimental——
Farewell!

译后小记

《沙扬娜拉——赠日本女郎》是新月派诗人徐志摩的佳作，"最是那一低头的温柔，像一朵水莲花不胜凉风的娇羞"，借被轻风吹拂的水莲花以物喻人，将日本女郎那娇羞动人，温婉含蓄的美生动呈现。"道一声珍重，道一声珍重"，女郎把内心复杂的情感化作一声声的"珍重"来表达自己对对方难以割舍的爱慕敬仰之情。诗题"沙扬娜拉"是日语"さようなら"（再会，再见）的音译，对应的英文"sayonara"是个音译词。英译这首诗时，为了诗篇连贯，并未将诗题译为"sayonara"，而是译为"farewell"，这是因为诗中"道一声珍重，道一声珍重"就是"沙扬娜拉"的代名词，换言之，"道一声珍重"和"沙扬娜拉"都是说"再见，保重"。透过"Fare thee well, Fare thee well"也似乎能再现日本女郎"道一声珍重，道一声珍重"的生动神情。罗伯特·彭斯（Robert Burns）在《红红的玫瑰》（*A Red Red Rose*）中有一句："And fare thee weel, my only luve!"其中"fare thee weel"即"farewell"（再见）。

6. 季候

徐志摩

他俩初起的日子,
像春风吹着春花。
花对风说:"我要",
风不回话:他给!

但春花早变了泥,
春风也不知去向。
她怨,说天时太冷;
"不久就冻冰,"他说。

6. *Season*

By Xu Zhimo

When they were together at the beginning
Like spring breeze caressing spring flowers.
"I want," said the flower to the wind.
The wind did not reply: he gave!

But the spring flowers has turned into mud,
The spring breeze has disappeared.
She complains that it is too cold;
"Soon it will freeze," he says.

译后小记

全诗的经典在于作者把季节的变换和情感的变化很巧妙地结合在一起。短短数字,两条"主线"都十分清晰,第一条:季节的变换,大自然的规律变换,由不得你来改变。第二条:情感的变化,所有的情感潜规则在这里都合理地暴露,由不得你不相信。

翻译时注意炼字,如"春风吹着春花"的"吹"不译"blow",而译为"caress";"春风也不知去向"用了"disappear"一词。

7. 消息

徐志摩

雷雨暂时收敛了；
双龙似的双虹，
显现在雾霭中，
夭矫，鲜艳，生动，——
好兆！明天准是好天了。

什么！又是一阵打雷，——
在云外，在天外，
又是一片暗淡，
不见了鲜虹彩，——
希望，不曾站稳，又毁了。

7. The Message

By Xu Zhimo

The thunderstorm has abated for the time being;
A double rainbow like a double dragon,
Appears in the mist,
Dainty, bright and vivid, —
Good sign! It must be a fine day tomorrow.

What! There comes another burst of thunder, —
Beyond the clouds, beyond the sky.
It is dark again.
Gone is the bright rainbow; —
Hope, a flash in the pan, disappears again.

译后小记

第一节，雷雨暂停，天上现彩虹，盼天晴；第二节，又闻云天外雷声，天又阴了。诗人采用对比手法，一喜一悲，戏剧性地展现出主人公因"消息"变化而内心惆怅的情感。

译诗还是在字里行间把握原诗的节奏和情感，读者可细细品味。

8. 教我如何不想她

刘半农

天上飘着些微云，
地上吹着些微风，
啊！
微风吹动了我的头发，
教我如何不想她？

月光恋爱着海洋，
海洋恋爱着月光。
啊！
这般蜜也似的银夜，
教我如何不想她？

水面落花慢慢流，
水底鱼儿慢慢游。
啊！
燕子你说些什么话？
教我如何不想她？

枯树在冷风里摇，
野火在暮色中烧。
啊！
西天还有些儿残霞，
教我如何不想她？

8. *How Can I Not Miss Her There*

By Liu Bannong

Some clouds float in the sky;
Over the land waft a breeze light.
Ah!
The breeze stirs my hair;
How can I not miss her there?

The moonlight loves the sea;
The sea loves the moonlight.
Ah!
The silver night, so sweet so fair,
How can I not miss her there?

Flowers float on the surface slowly;
Fishes swim in the water leisurely.
Ah!
Swallow, what do you murmur?
How can I not miss her there?

Withered trees in wind are shivering;
Wildfires in the twilight are burning.
Ah!
The west sky glows a last flare;
How can I not miss her there?

译后小记

《教我如何不想她》于1920年9月4日创作于伦敦,原题为《情歌》;1926年9月收入北京北新书局出版的新诗集《扬鞭集》,改题为《教我如何不想她》。诗作表达了一个海外游子对祖国"母亲"的眷恋之情,每节诗以"教我如何不想她"收尾,更标志着汉语第三人称女性代词"她"字的诞生。

原诗八对诗行都押全韵,体现原诗的主流押韵;运用重复、拟人修辞格;译诗注意流畅自然之感,情真意切,有一定的韵律和节奏,并保留原诗拟人修辞格,如"Swallow, what do you murmur?"原诗的重复修辞,一咏三叹,在译诗中也得以再现。

9. 窗外

康白情

窗外的闲月，
紧恋着窗内蜜也似的相思。
相思都恼了，
她还涎着脸儿在墙上相窥。

回头月也恼了，
一抽身儿就没了，
月倒没了；
相思倒觉着舍不得了。

9. *Outside the Window*

By Kang Baiqing

The leisure Moon outside,
Adheres closely to the sooth Lovesick inside.
Until he's annoyed,
She keeps peering on the wall and grinning cheekily.

The Moon is annoyed too in a while,
And disappears abruptly.
Gone is the Moon,
But the Lovesick actually feel reluctant to part.

译后小记

这是一首别有情趣的爱情小诗,写的是"闲月"和"相思"的一场恋情误会。全诗分为两节。诗的第一节,写"闲月"紧恋着"相思",她把"相思"给弄恼了,仍然"涎着脸儿",她深爱着对方,她实在不知道"相思"有什么苦恼。诗的第二节,写"闲月"恋"相思",却落得个"多情却被无情恼",于是"月"也恼了,一抽身儿气恼地离开了。但"相思"不是无情物,"闲月"一走,"相思"又舍不得了。

拙译将"闲月"和"相思"拟人化来译,故大写"Moon","Lovesickness",采用人称代词"she""he"来指代,并用"peering""grinning"等拟人化动词,尽量呈现出这月夜下相思的画面。

10. 小诗

王统照

多年的秋灯之前,
一夕的温软之语,
如今随著飞尘散去,
不知那时的余音,
又落在谁的心里?

10. *A Little Poem*

By Wang Tongzhao

Years ago, in autumn in a dim light,
An affectionate talk for a whole night
Is gone with dust now;
The lingering sound in the past
On whose heart will echo and last?

译后小记

从原诗中的几个意象"秋灯""软语""余音"等,初步理解这是一首怀念昔日朦胧情感的小诗,诗歌说话人"我"追忆多年前的灯下爱语。当年的爱语犹在耳畔,Ta 却弃"我"而去,不知如今跟谁在一起重复着"我们"曾经爱的耳语?

"秋灯"一词颇有诗意，文人墨客也多以此词入诗，营造了一种淡淡的忧伤和朦胧的意境，故这里的"灯"译为"in dim light"；"温软之语"理解为情侣之间的私话，故这里译为"an affectionate talk"。

全诗五行，前三行，回忆过去，感慨现在，诗人心中有些许失落，其核心内容是"……温软之语如今随著飞尘散去"，故用一个现在时态的句子"An affectionate talk is gone with dust now"；后两行是追问，故译为一个将来时态的问句："The lingering sound…on whose heart will echo and last?" "我"心底挥之不去的声音（曾经爱的耳语）又会在谁的心底回响呢？译诗用了"last"一词，不仅是为了押韵，更是耐人寻味。

11. 不足之感

朱自清

他是太阳，
我像一枝烛光；
他是海，浩浩荡荡的，
我像他的细流；
他是锁着的摩云塔，
我像塔下徘徊者。

他像鸟儿，有美丽的歌声，
在天空里自在飞着；
又像花儿，有鲜艳的颜色，
在乐园里盛开着；
我不曾有什么，
只好暗地里待着了。

11. *Insufficiency*

By Zhu Ziqing

He is the sun,
While I'm a candle;
He is a formidable sea,
While I'm a mere trickle;

He is a skyscraping tower,
Around which I am a stroller.

He is a bird with adulcet voice
Flying at will in the blue sky,
A flower with bright color
Blooming in the garden;
Cause I own nothing,
I'd better stay in private.

译后小记

《不足之感》是现代作家朱自清于 1920 年 10 月 3 日创作的一首现代诗。这首诗共两节，第一节用太阳与烛光之比，海与细流之比，摩云塔与塔下的徘徊者之比，在自谦中褒扬了前者；在第二节中，又温情地将鸟儿于天空歌唱，花儿乐园之美，赞美于"他"，至于自己，他没有再说些什么，他只是暗暗地自我努力，期待着与"他"达到同一高度。

原诗采用的是一种对称式比喻的排比结构，或称作双向博喻结构，笔者翻译时注意句子结构的对比关系。英语是曲折语，名词、形容词往往可以通过词形变化表示，故少用范畴词；而汉语没有词形的曲折变化，一般会在词尾加上范畴词，如诗题"不足之感"中"……之感"即为范畴词，翻译时，只须译出名词"insufficiency"，无须译出范畴词"feeling"；同理，"陌生感""新鲜感"译为"strangeness""freshness"。

12. 光明

朱自清

风雨沉沉的夜里,
前面一片荒郊。
走尽荒郊,
便是人们的道。

呀！黑暗里歧路万千,
叫我怎样走好？
"上帝！快给我些光明罢,
让我好向前跑！"

上帝慌着说,"光明？
我没处给你找！
你要光明,
你自己去造！"

12. *Light*

By Zhu Ziqing

In a stormy night,
Ahead a vast wasteland stretches away.
At the end of the wilderness,
There lies the human way.

Ah! There are so many cross-roads in the dark.
Which one shall I set foot on?
"God! Please give me some light!
Let me move on!"

God answered promptly, "Light?
I can find it nowhere!
If you need light,
Make it yourself somewhere!

译后小记

此诗是现代作家、诗人朱自清于1919年创作的一首现代诗。此诗表达了时为北京大学哲学系学生的诗人，对光明社会的憧憬，对新的人生道路的向往。此诗通过假设与"上帝"答问的方式，运用象征和对比，把追求光明的哲理融入形象之中，避免了抽象与晦涩之感。

全诗十二行，分为三个层次，每个层次都是四行。诗的第一节，写的是作者对于现实社会和民族前途的看法。第二节写道："黑暗里歧路万千，/叫我怎样走好？"第三段假借"上帝"的答问，说明光明必须靠自己去创造。

第一节，"风雨沉沉"，译者理解"风雨"是一个词，选择"stormy"，而不是"windy and rainy"；"荒郊"第一次用"a vast wasteland"，第二次用"the wilderness"来避免重复；"人们的道"是隐喻"新的人生道路"，故译为"the human way"。

第二节，"叫我怎样走好"，译者按原诗的认知译为"Which one shall I set foot on?"（踏足那条路）而没有改用"Which one shall I take?"（选择那条路），从而突出"走"（set foot on）。

第三节,"要光明"是"需要光明",而不是"想要",前面已经交代了背景,故译者选择"need"。

这首诗好懂好译,但不容易译好。虽是现代自由诗,原诗有其音韵节奏,每节行尾押韵 abcb,译诗紧跟其音韵和节奏,选择流畅自然的语言表达。

13. 秋晨

于赓虞

别了，星霜漫天的黑夜，
我受了圣水难洗的苦孽，
你方从我的背上踏过，
欢迎啊，东曙，你又已复活！

在这最后的瞬间，我睁眼
双手抱住太阳的脚，看
叶颤，花舞，听市声沉醉，
直到落下欢欣的眼泪！

13. *Autumn Morning*

By Yu Gengyu

Goodbye, so long frosty starry night!
I've suffered what holy water can't make it right
Before you step over my back and survive.
Welcome! East Dawn, again you revive!

In the last moment, I open my eyes in delight,
Holding the sun's feet in my arms, gazing at light
Leaves quivering, flowers dancing, and I listen to the voices
Babbling in the market, till I shed tears of joy.

译后小记

  汉语的流水句如何分句、断句是这首诗翻译的一个难点。

  第一节着重抒写告别秋夜的心情，以此反衬对秋晨的企盼和欢迎。第一句告别秋夜，独立成句，"星霜漫天"显得秋夜凄冷而漫长。第二句中"我受了圣水难洗的苦辜，你方从我的背上踏过"，措辞别出心裁，富有暗示性，翻译时找到"before"一词是关键。第三句欢迎"东曙"，"东曙"类似人名，大写，拟人化，译为"east dawn"，如译"east morning rays"则意义更为确切，但略显冗长。

  第二节正面抒写了作者面对秋晨的心情。第一句，"东曙"即"秋晨曙光"到来的一瞬间，"我"睁眼。第二句，"太阳的脚"指太阳射进室内的光线，"双手抱住太阳的脚"，喻指张开双臂拥抱阳光，英译保留"太阳的脚"意象不变，但"双手"不宜译"hands"，而译为"arms"。接着一连串动作写视觉和听觉印象，"我"看到枝叶和花朵在秋风中摇摆，觉得它们是激动地颤抖，欢乐地舞蹈，都在欢庆终于摆脱了黑夜的折磨；听到闹嚷嚷的市声，"我"不觉得嘈杂，却"沉醉"直到欢欣落泪。这都是"我"心情的外化，无形的情绪和心理活动则隐含其中。

  原诗运用了拟人化的笔触，译诗的选词措字也应更加注意。原诗押韵格式为 aabb，译诗同样押韵。

14. 再生

潘漠华

我想在我底心野,
再摘拢荒草与枯枝,
寥廓苍茫的天宇下,
重新烧起几堆野火。

我想在将天明时我的生命,
再吹起我嘹亮的画角,
重招拢满天的星,
重画出满天的云彩。

我想停唱我底挽歌,
想在我底挽歌内,
完全消失去我自己,
也完全再生我自己。

14. *Rebirth*

By Pan Mohua

I'd like to regather from the wilderness of my heart
Some wild weeds and withered branches.
Under the boundless sky
To relight a few wildfires.

I'd like once more in my life, before the dawn,
To blow loudly my horn again,
To recall on stars over the vault of heaven,
To redraw colorful clouds all over the sky.

I'd like to stop singing my elegy,
I'd like in my heart
To disappear myself completely,
And to revive myself wholly.

译后小记

诗题"再生"译为"rebirth",有"新生""复活""轮回"之意。文中"再生"用了"revive",避免重复。

原诗三节,每节是完整一句话,全诗用了三个平行结构"我想……"。从"重新烧起几堆野火","再吹起我嘹亮的画角",再到"完全消失去我自己",仿佛凤凰涅槃一般,层层递进,译诗采用三个"I'd like…"对应来译。

第一节和第二节,诗人反复用到"再""重",为避免重复单调,译诗采用多种方式来表达,如在动词前加前缀"re-",如"regather""relight""recall""redraw",或用副词"once more""again"。

英语句子只有一个主动词,译诗将句中第一个"想做的动作"作为主动词,其他的化为不定式短语表目的的形式。

15. 早寒

梁实秋

遭了秋神谪贬的红叶,
漫地飞舞起来,空剩
那瘦骨嶙嶙的干树枝,
收殓着再世荣华的梦。

宇宙线像座斑驳的废堡,
处处显露已往的遗痕,
诱使载满悲哀的诗心,
痛苦命尽途穷的黄昏!

15. *Early Chill*

By Liang Shiqiu

Rusted leaves banished by the autumn god
Flying away to the ground, there left simply
Bare bony branches
With a dream of another glorious life.

Cosmic lines look like cracks on a mottled castle
With traces of past revealed everywhere,
Tempting a sorrowful poetic heart
And a painful exhausting dusk!

译后小记

遭了秋神谪贬的"红叶",已经成衰败颓丧之势,故不译"red leaves"而译为"rusted leaves";那瘦骨嶙嶙的干树枝,用了押头韵的三个词"bare bony branches"来凸显;现代汉语诗歌英译,须将"竹节"式汉语转换成"大树"型英语,找准主干,再添枝加叶,确保译诗流畅自然。

16. 断章

卞之琳

你站在桥上看风景，
看风景的人在楼上看你。
明月装饰了你的窗子，
你装饰了别人的梦。

16. *Fragment*

By Bian Zhilin

On the bridge your eyes feast the view;
On the tower the viewers admire you.
The moon bedecks your window neat;
While you adorn another dream sweet.

译后小记

《断章》是现代诗人卞之琳于1935年创作的一首现代诗歌。诗人通过对"风景"的刹那间感悟，涉及了"相对性"的哲理命题。

这首诗已有不少名家翻译，尽量找寻自己的表达方式。首句"你站在桥上看风景"，两个动作，化为一个介词短语"on the bridge"，一个小句"your eyes feast the view"（你的眼睛饱览风景）；第二句"看风景的人在楼上看你"，这个"楼"理解为观景的"塔楼"，"看你"因为你已经在他们欣赏的风景之中，故将"看"译为"admire"；第三句"明月装饰了你的窗子"和第四句"你装饰了别人的梦"，译者根据语境，分别增加了两个形容词"neat""sweat"作补语，"neat"有"整洁，美好"之意，说得通，"sweat"一词添加合理。另外，"neat""sweat"都是闭口音，是否透着月夜与梦境的轻柔之美呢？

全诗音韵节奏尚可，行尾押韵 aabb。

17. 你是人间的四月天

林徽因

我说你是人间的四月天；
笑响点亮了四面风；
轻灵在春的光艳中交舞着变。

你是四月早天里的云烟，
黄昏吹着风的软，
星子在无意中闪，
细雨点洒在花前。

那轻，那娉婷，你是，鲜妍
百花的冠冕你戴着；
你是天真，庄严；
你是夜夜的月圆。

雪化后那片鹅黄，你像；
新鲜初放芽的绿，你是；
柔嫩，喜悦
水光浮动着你梦中期待的白莲。

你是一树一树的花开，
是燕在梁间呢喃，
——你是爱，是暖，是希望；
你是人间的四月天！

17. *You Are the April Day in the World*

By Lin Huiyin

You are the April Day in the world, I'd say
Your giggles brighten up all the winds aye
Tinkling in the spring light to play

You are the mist of the early April day
At dusk soft breezes sway
The stars blink unconscious ray
The drizzles over the flowers spray

So light, so lithe you are
Gorgeous crown of flowers you wear
In an innocent and solemn way
You are the full moon night by night

The light yellow after snow, you seem
The fresh green of a sprout, you are
So delicate, so delight
In the water floats your fantastic white lily

You are blossoms of the trees
Twitter of the swallows on the beams
—You are love, you are warmth, you are hope
You are in the world the April day

译后小记

此诗是林徽因于1934年创作的一首现代诗。第一节写出"四月天"这一意象，写出了春风轻灵、春光明媚、春色多变等四月天的季候特征；第二节至第四节则分别以四月天中各种不同的具象来比喻生活中的各种画面；最后诗人直抒情意，概言"你"就是"爱"，就是"暖"，就是"希望"。

第一节，"我说"译为"I'd say"（我想说），为的是加入一种情感表达，比"I say"（我说）委婉；"笑响点亮了四面风"，一定是欢愉的笑声，故译为"giggles"；"点亮"也是比喻，本可译为"light up"，但接下来的"春的光艳中"用到"spring light"，故译为"brighten up"；"轻灵在春的光艳中交舞着变"，这一句写春风，怎样译出"轻灵"，译者采用转喻，以春风轻灵而过的"脚步声"来译，"交舞着变"不好直译，暂且译为"play"。

第二节，"云烟"理解为一个词，译为"mist"；第二节的"云烟""风的软""星子的散""洒向花前的细雨点"都是"四月天"具体的意象。

第三节，"轻"是"light"，"娉婷"，婀娜多姿，译者找来押头韵的"lithe"（轻盈）来译；"百花"并非百朵花，译为"flowers"；"你是天真，庄严"理解为头戴花冠时，你的模样，故译为"in an innocent and solemn way"。

第四节，汉语多用动词，英语少用动词，动词"化""放"都不译；"柔嫩，喜悦"还是找押头韵的两个词来译；"梦中期待的"化为形容词"fantastic"，省去动词"期待"。

第五节，"你是爱，是暖，是希望"，中文的"你"只出现一次，译为英语，需要多加"you"，才更能表达出炙热的情感。

18. 时间

林徽因

人间的季候永远不断在转变
春时你留下多处残红,翩然辞别,
本不想回来时同谁叹息秋天!

现在连秋云黄叶又已失落去
辽远里,剩下灰色的长空一片
透彻的寂寞,你忍听冷风独语?

18. *Time*

By Lin Huiyin

The seasons on earth are forever changing;
Leaving fade flowers in spring, you bade farewell lightly,
With no intention of sighing when back in fall!

Now even the autumn clouds and yellow leaves are gone.
In vast space, there left a gray sky.
In loneliness, can you bear the cold wind solo?

译后小记

原诗每一诗行，不算行中的标点符号，除第二行为十三个字外，其余都是十二个字；英译诗中每一诗行，除第二行为十三个音节外，其余都是十二个音节，大致整齐对应。

诗人借"人间的季候……转变"，表达对"你"的思念。"残红""黄叶""灰色的长空"看似颜色斑斓，留在诗人心中的都是萧瑟和怅惘，"叹息""寂寞""冷风独语"都是孤独的基调。翻译这首诗，想到的是原文的意境和译文的连贯。

译诗中，"残红"用了押头韵的两个单词"fade flowers"来表达，"黄叶"译为"yellow leaves"，"冷风独语"译为"the cold wind solo"，与诗歌情绪基调一致。

汉语动词连用，如"忍听"，翻译成英语时，有时只须译出一个动词即可，这里的"听"就省去没译。

19. 无题

林徽因

什么时候再能有
那一片静；
溶溶在春风中立着，
面对着山，面对着小河流？

什么时候还能那样
满掬着希望；
披拂新绿，耳语似的诗思，
登上城楼，更听那一声钟响？

什么时候，又什么时候，心
才真能懂得
这时间的距离；山河的年岁；
昨天的静，钟声
昨天的人
怎样又在今天里划下一道影！

19. *Untitled*

By Lin Huiyin

When shall we have it again,
The tranquility—

Standing in the spring breeze,
Facing the hills, facing the rills?

When shall we have it again,
The full hope—
With a fresh poetic inspiration
Going up to the tower to listen to the bell?

When, but when, the heart
Shall really understand
The distance of time, the time of hills and rills?
How shall the tranquility of yore, the bell of yore
And the one of yore
Leave a trace today?!

译后小记

此诗节奏鲜明,意境悠远。翻译的难点在于如何理解原诗和诗意再现。第一小节,后两行是"静"的具体呈现;第二小节,后两行是"希望"的具体呈现,译诗采用同样的句式,同样的节奏;第三节,层层推进,表达心底一抹长叹,译诗当再现此结构和意境。

20. 情愿

林徽因

我情愿化成一片落叶，
让风吹雨打到处飘零；
或流云一朵，在澄蓝天，
和大地再没有些牵连。

但抱紧那伤心的标志，
去触遇没着落的怅惘；
在黄昏，夜半，蹑着脚走，
全是空虚，再莫有温柔；

忘掉曾有这世界；有你；
哀悼谁又曾有过爱恋；
落花似的落尽，忘了去
这些个泪点里的情绪。

到那天一切都不存留，
比一闪光，一息风更少
痕迹，你也要忘掉了我
曾经在这世界里活过。

20. *I Would Rather*

By Lin Huiyin

I would rather be a fallen leaf,

Drifting about in the wind and rain;

Or be a floating cloud in the blue sky,

Detached from the ground;

Holding tight to the heart-shattered sign,

To contact the hopeless affections in bygones;

In the dusk or at midnight, tiptoeing back

To the void world, absurd and cold;

To forget the existence of the world, and of you,

Bemoaning as if we had ever loved;

To fade away like a falling flower, forgetting

All the sentiments in my tears;

Nothing would be left till that day,

Less than a fleeting ray or a passing breath of wind

A trail, and you should forget me,

Forget the world I ever lived too.

译后小记

这首诗于1931年9月被发表于《新月诗选》。原诗一诗四节，自然流畅。诗中"再没有些牵连""再莫有温柔""忘掉曾有这世界""忘掉了我"这一类拒绝之词，是诗人内心对"你"的独白，委婉拒绝"你"的情意，"飘零""怅惘""空虚"流露了诗人心底淡淡的不舍。翻译此诗，尽量保持自然流畅，真实传递诗人的内在情感。前面三小节，主干都是"我情愿……"，翻译时须注意结构的完整和语言的流畅；最后一节是对"你"的告别，主干是"你也要忘掉了我……"。译诗仍然一诗四节，处理成两个语法完整的句子。

21. 八月的忧愁

林徽因

黄水塘里游着白鸭,

高粱梗油青的刚高过头,

这跳动的心怎样安插,

田里一窄条路,八月里这忧愁?

天是昨夜雨洗过的,山岗

照着太阳又留一片影;

羊跟着放羊的转进村庄,

一大棵树荫下罩着井,又像是心!

从没有人说过八月什么话,

夏天过去了,也不到秋天。

但我望着田垄,土墙上的瓜,

仍不明白生活同梦怎样的连牵。

21. *August Blues*

By Lin Huiyin

White ducks swim in the yellow pond;

The green sorghum stalks are just a bit higher than me.

Where shall I place my pounding heart,

A narrow road in the field, or the August blues?

The sky was washed by the rain last night; the sun

Shines over the hills with some shadows left;

The sheep follow the shepherd into the village;

Under the shade of a big tree lies a well, like a heart!

No one ever said anything about August;

Summer has passed, and it is not yet autumn.

Gazing at the fields and the melons on the earthen wall,

I still don't understand how life and dream are linked.

译后小记

《八月的忧愁》被认为是一首优美的田园诗,发表于1936年。"不明白生活同梦怎样的连牵"一句即透露了诗人的愁思之深:浪漫的理想与现实为什么竟有如此落差。在安静、幽美的田园风光背景下,潜藏着诗人深深的思考和难以解脱的愁绪。这种思考过程即是女性生命意识觉醒的过程,但觉醒的过程充满苦恼与焦虑。

22. 笑

林徽因

笑的是她的眼睛，口唇，
和唇边浑圆的旋涡。
艳丽如同露珠，
朵朵的笑向
贝齿的闪光里躲。
那是笑——神的笑，美的笑：
水的映影，风的轻歌。

笑的是她惺松的鬓发，
散乱的挨着她的耳朵。
轻软如同花影，
痒痒的甜蜜
涌进了你的心窝。
那是笑——诗的笑，画的笑：
云的留痕，浪的柔波。

22. *Smiles*

By Lin Huiyin

Smiling are her eyes, her lips,
And the round dimple by the lips.

Gorgeous as dew,

Blossoming smiles

Are hiding toward the glistening teeth.

It is a smile—of god, of beauty:

The reflection in the water, the song in the wind.

Smiling are her loose curls,

Sprawling against her ears.

Soft as a flower,

Crispy sweet smiles

Flood into your heart.

It is a smile—of poetry, of painting:

Traces of a cloud, ripples of a wave.

译后小记

　　此诗通篇描绘的是一个少女高雅纯洁的笑，诗中用诸多女性的意象展现了笑的美好，在露珠与花影间，阳光的气息扑面而来；在轻歌和柔波中，纯粹的美丽尽现眼前。

　　译诗呈现原诗的意象美和结构美，或曰建筑美。

23. 深夜里听到乐声

林徽因

这一定又是你的手指，
轻弹着，
在这深夜，稠密的悲思；

我不禁颊边泛上了红，
静听着，
这深夜里弦子的生动。

一声听从我心底穿过，
忒凄凉
我懂得，但我怎能应和？

生命早描定她的式样，
太薄弱
是人们的美丽的想象。

除非在梦里有这么一天，
你和我
同来攀动那根希望的弦。

23. *The Music I Hear Late at Night*

By Lin Huiyin

It must be your fingers again,

Plucking lightly,

At a deep night, deep sad thoughts;

I cannot help blushing,

Listening silently

To the vividness of the strings at night.

A sound runs through my heart,

So desolate;

I know, but how can I echo?

Life has made her pattern;

So weak

Are people's fancies.

Unless in a dream one day,

You and I

Touch the chord of hope together.

译后小记

这首诗于 1931 年 9 月发表于《新月诗选》。此诗用细腻真挚的笔触，展现了一种难以言状的爱的隐痛，男子的相思，女子的惆怅跃然纸上，表达了一种婉转而悲伤的心情。这首诗描写的虽然只是普通的儿女情长，但是又仿若古人的"余音袅袅，不绝如缕"，细细品读，令人心感其伤。

第一小节，"你"的手指轻轻弹拨琴弦，但琴音里分明透着"稠密悲思"，翻译时，也须注意这两者的搭配，故译为"plucking…deep sad thoughts"；最后一节，除非梦里你我"攀动"这那根希望的弦，套用英语习语"strike/touch a chord"（触动心弦）来译。

原诗一诗五节，一节一韵，一节三句，两长一短，错落有致，节奏相当，极具音乐美和建筑美。译诗不押韵，但尽力再现原诗情感，还原部分美感。

24. 仍然

林徽因

你舒伸得象一湖水向着晴空里
白云，又象是一流冷涧，澄清
许我循着林岸穷究你的泉源：
我却仍然怀抱着百般的疑心
对你的每一个映影！

你展开象个千瓣的花朵！
鲜妍是你的每一瓣，更有芳沁，
那温存袭人的花气，伴着晚凉：
我说花儿，这正是春的捉弄人，
来偷取人们的痴情！

你又学叶叶的书篇随风吹展，
揭示你的每一个深思；每一角心境，
你的眼睛望着我，不断的在说话：
我却仍然没有回答，一片的沉静
永远守住我的魂灵。

24. *As Usual*

By Lin Huiyin

Thou stretch like a lake reflecting in the blue sky

A cloud, like a gurgling stream too, clear and clean.
May I follow the shore to thy fountain:
I still harbor every suspicion
To each shadow of thee!

Thou spread out like a flower with a thousand pedals!
Gorgeous is each of thy petals, with fragrance,
The sweet flower in a cool evening:
Flower, I say, it is the trick of spring
To steal people's love!

Thou pretend the book leaves being blown in the wind,
Revealing thy thought, thy mind.
Thy eyes look at me and keep saying:
Still I did not answer; The silence
Keeps my soul forever.

译后小记

这首诗写于1931年，可以看作是林徽因对徐志摩《偶然》的应答之作。诗人表明心迹，委婉表达自己的情感态度。一诗三节，结构类似，颇具建筑之美。

25. 山中一个夏夜

林徽因

山中一个夏夜，深得
象没有底一样；
黑影，松林密密的；
周围没有点光亮。
对山闪着只一盏灯——两盏
象夜的眼，夜的眼在看！

满山的风全蹑着脚
象是走路一样；
躲过了各处的枝叶
各处的草，不响。
单是流水，不断的在山谷上
石头的心，石头的口在唱。

均匀的一片静，罩下
象张软垂的幔帐。
疑问不见了，四角里
模糊，是梦在窥探？
夜象在祈祷，无声的在期望
幽郁的虔诚在无声里布漫。

25. *A Summer Night in the Mountains*

By Lin Huiyin

A summer night in the mountains, deep

As if there were no bottom;

Dark shadows, dense pines;

There is no light around.

A single lamp or two flash over the mountain

Like the eyes of the night, gazing!

The wind crepts all over the mountain

Like tiptoeing;

To dodge each branch

Each grass, quietly.

Only the gurgling water sings constantly on the valley

On the heart of the stone, on the mouth of the stone.

An even piece of quiet hangs over

Like a soft dangling curtain.

I am wondering, in every corner

Fuzzy, is the dream prying?

The night seems praying in silence;

The piety of deep gloom pervades in silence.

译后小记

诗人运用比喻、拟人等修辞手法来写山中夏夜,如"……灯……象夜的眼,夜的眼在看","风全蹑着脚……躲过了各处的枝叶",夏夜因而生动有趣。翻译时注意选词措字,如第二节"The wind crepts all over the mountain /Like tiptoeing;/To dodge each branch",笔者有意选择了"crepts over""tiptoeing""dodge"以再现山中夏夜的风。

26. 记忆

林徽因

断续的曲子，最美或最温柔的
夜，带着一天的星。
记忆的梗上，谁不有
两三朵娉婷，披着情绪的花
无名的展开
野荷的香馥，
每一瓣静处的月明。

湖上风吹过，头发乱了，或是
水面皱起象鱼鳞的锦。
四面里的辽阔，如同梦
荡漾着心中彷徨的过往
不着痕迹，谁都
认识那图画，
沉在水底记忆的倒影！

26. *Memory*

By Lin Huiyin

Intermittent music, in a most beautiful
Night, flies with the stars all over the sky.

Deep in the memory, who does not have

Two or three delicate emotional flowers

Expanding with no reason

The fragrance of a wild lotus

Pedal by pedal in the moonlight.

The breeze blows over the lake, stirring the hair, or

The surface of water wrinkled like fish scales.

The vastness in every side is like a dream

Rippling of the wandering past

Without a trace. Everyone

Knows the picture,

Sinking in the water the reflection of memory!

译后小记

"记忆的梗上,谁不有两三朵娉婷,披着情绪的花无名的展开",这首诗是作者心底悠长的回忆,翻译时需要注意把握这种意境和情感。

27. 题剔空菩提叶

林徽因

认得这透明体,
智慧的叶子掉在人间?
消沉,慈净——
那一天一闪冷焰,
一叶无声的坠地,
仅证明了智慧寂寞
孤零的终会死在风前!
昨天又昨天,美
还逃不出时间的威严;
相信这里睡眠着最美丽的
骸骨,一丝魂魄月边留念,——
……
菩提树下清荫则是去年!

27. Ode to a Hollow Bodi Leaf

By Lin Huiyin

Recognize the transparent thing,
A leaf of wisdom falling on earth?
Depression, Cleanness—
There flashed a cool flame that day,

A leaf fell silently to the ground,
Proving the loneliness of wisdom only.
The lonely one will die in front of the wind!
Yesterday by yesterday, beauty
Could never escape from the dignity of time;
Believe it, there sleeps the most beautiful
Skeleton, a soul lingering around the moon—
……
Under the Bodi tree the shade was last year!

译后小记

原诗生动细腻，充满禅意。写飘零的落叶，却在这片叶子身上赋予诗人太多的情思与哲思，细读之下，仿佛令人进入一种空濛的禅境，其中自有一份迷人的诗情。译诗就像临摹这一幅禅意之画。

28. 静坐

林徽因

冬有冬的来意，
寒冷像花，——
花有花香，冬有回忆一把。
一条枯枝影，青烟色的瘦细，
在午后的窗前拖过一笔画；
寒里日光淡了，渐斜…
就是那样地
像待客人说话
我在静沉中默啜着茶。

28. *Meditation*

By Lin Huiyin

Winter has its purpose,
Cold as a flower, —
Flowers have sweet odors, winter memories.
A shadow of a dead branch, thin and smoky,
Strokes across the window in the afternoon;
The sun glimmers cold, gradually slanting…
Just in the way
Waiting my guest to break the ice
I sip my tea in silence.

译后小记

此诗写于1936年11月,原载于1937年1月31日《大公报文艺副刊》。以个人情绪的起伏和波澜为主题,静坐沉思,探索生活和爱的哲理,诗句委婉柔丽,韵律自然。

29. 那一晚

林徽因

那一晚你的船推出了河心，
澄蓝的天上托着密密的星。
那一晚你的手牵着我的手，
迷惘的星夜封锁起重愁。
那一晚你和我分定了方向，
两人各认取个生活的模样。

到如今我的船仍然在海面飘，
细弱的桅杆常在风涛里摇。
到如今太阳只在我背后徘徊，
层层的阴影留守在我周围。
到如今我还记着那一晚的天，
星光，眼泪，白茫茫的江边！
到如今我还想念你岸上的耕种：
红花儿黄花儿朵朵的生动。

那一晚我希望要走到了顶层，
蜜一般酿出那记忆的滋润。
那一天我要挎上带羽翼的弓箭，
望着你花园里射一个满弦，
那一天你要听到鸟般的歌唱，
那便是我静候着你的赞赏。

那一天你要看到零乱的花影,

那便是我私闯入当年的边境。

29. That Night

By Lin Huiyin

That night your boat was pushed out of the river;
The clear blue sky set off the dense stars.
That night your hand took mine;
The lost starry night blocked the melancholy.
That night you and I set the direction;
Each took his own way.

So far, my boat is still afloat on the water,
Whose weak mast often shakes in the wind.
So far, the sun lingers only behind me,
With layers of shadows around me.
So far, I still remember the sky of that night,
Starlight, tears, and the vast river!
So far, I still think of your cultivation on the shore:
Each flower, red or yellow, were blossoming lively.

That night I wish to get to the acme,
Producing a wisp of memory sweet as honey.
That day I will carry a bow and arrow with wings,

Watching you pull a full string in your garden;

That day you will hear the song of a bird,

What I await your appreciation.

That day you will see the shadow of flowers in disorder,

When I broke into the border.

译后小记

《那一晚》可以说是林徽因对一段隐秘情感的真实、细腻的回溯，原载于1931年4月《诗刊》第2期（署名：尺棰）。诗人用隽婉、纤丽的笔调向读者敞开自己的内心世界，我们可以感到作者是如何轻溯这虽已过去但仍萦绕在心的神圣、纯洁的精神边境。

30. 一首桃花

林徽因

桃花，
那一树的嫣红，
像是春说的一句话：
朵朵露凝的娇艳，
是一些
玲珑的字眼，
一瓣瓣的光致，
又是些
柔的匀的吐息；
含着笑，
在有意无意间
生姿的顾盼。
看，——
那一颤动在微风里
她又留下，淡淡的，
在三月的薄唇边，
一瞥，
一瞥多情的痕迹！

30. *Ode to Peach Blossoms*

By Lin Huiyin

Peach blossoms,
A tree of crimson,
Look like what spring said:

Each blossom with dew

Is some

Exquisite words,

Each delicate petal

A breath

Soft and even;

With a smile

Intentionally or unintentionally

Displaying its charm.

Look!—

That one quivering in the breeze

Leaves again faintly

On the thin lips of march

A glance,

A glimpse of amorous signs!

译后小记

"朵朵露凝的娇艳,是一些玲珑的字眼",这种美让人怦然心动,让人忍不住去细读。此诗是近现代新月派诗人林徽因于1931年创作的一首新诗。以"桃花"开篇,描绘了自然景物桃花之美;而后引入"春",将春与花融为一体,拟作一位顾盼生姿的曼妙女子。诗人用笔巧妙,以舒缓、轻柔的语调写尽桃花婀娜妩媚之态,读来如沐桃风,身心愉悦。

31. 诗的葬礼

洛夫

把一首
在抽屉里锁了三十年的情诗
投入火中
字
被烧得吱吱大叫
灰烬一言不发
它相信
总有一天
那人将在风中读到

31. *Funeral of a Poem*

By Luofu

A love poem

Locked in the drawer for thirty years

Is thrown into fire

With words

Wailing

Ash in silence

Believing

One day

Someone will read it in the wind

译后小记

这是一首尽得孤绝之美的佳作,全诗两节九行四十八字,结构精巧,感情动人,充满意象。翻译时,笔者注意用词的简约,语意的连贯流畅,译诗一气呵成,共两节九行三十词,连起来是一个完整的句子:"A love poem locked in the drawer for thirty years is thrown into fire, with words wailing, ash in silence, believing one day someone will read it in the wind."

原诗不加标点,译诗同样不用标点,这样诗意显得更加流畅。英文葡萄藤式的句式结构、单复数和冠词、介词等细节的运用有讲究,如:"with"带有"words"和"ash"两个宾语等。

32. 笑的种子

李广田

把一粒笑的种子
深深地种在心底,
纵是块忧郁的土地,
也滋长了这一粒种子。

笑的种子发了芽,
笑的种子又开了花,
花开在颤着的树叶里,
也开在道旁的浅草里。

尖塔的十字架上
开着笑的花,
飘在天空的白云里
也开着笑的花。

播种者现在何所呢,
那个流浪的小孩子?
永记得你那偶然的笑,
虽然不知道你的名字。

32. *The Seed of Laughter*

By Li Guangtian

A seed of laughter is sown
Deep in my heart;

A melancholy land as it is,
The seed is nurtured too.

The seed of laughter sprouts;
The seed of laughter blooms then,
Smiling among the quivering leaves,
Smiling in the shallow grass by the roadsides.

On the cross of the minaret
Smiling flowers are in bloom;
On the clouds in the sky,
Smiling flowers are in bloom too.

Where is the sower,
The wandering child?
I always remember your casual smile,
Although I don't know your name.

译后小记

这是一首有温度的诗，笑的种子可以发芽、开花。

汉语多无主句，是谁种下笑的种子呢？第一小节不知是"你"还是"我"；诗的最后一节，"播种者"原来是"那个流浪的小孩"。笔者注意译诗的语意连贯、语法完整，根据上下文确定词义，如第二节的"又"，笔者译为"then"，而不是"again"；最后一节"偶然的笑"，笔者译为"casual smile"，而不是"occasional smile"。

33. 雨景

朱湘

我心爱的雨景也多着呀；
春夜春梦时窗前的淅沥；
急雨点打上蕉叶的声音；
雾一般拂着人脸的雨丝；
从电光中泼下来的雷雨——
但将雨时的天我最爱了。
它虽然是灰色的却透明；
它蕴着一种无声的期待。
并且从云气中，不知哪里，
飘来了一声清脆的鸟啼。

33. The Scenes of Rain

By Zhu Xiang

Oh, there are so many scenes of rain I adore:
A pattering rain on windows on a spring night,
A furious shower on banana leaves with might,
A mist of drizzle stroking the face gently,
A thunderstorm poured from the lightning heavily—
Oh, but the sky is something I can't love more.
Grey but transparent before the upcoming rain;

A sign silent and imminent it does contain.
And from the clouds, I don't know where,
Comes a bird's crisp twitter over there.

译后小记

《雨景》是现代诗人朱湘于1924年11月22日创作的一首新诗，充分体现了新月派诗人所倡导的诗歌要有"音乐美、绘画美、建筑美"等主张。

全诗共十行，洋溢着一种明朗快乐的情调。前五行诗写了"心爱的雨景"的种种情态，既描摹了雨景，又寄寓了心情，可谓情与景高度融合。"淅沥"的春雨，给人快慰；雾般轻柔的"雨丝"拂面，引人遐思；"电光雷雨"急打芭蕉，催人奋进；"从电光中泼下来的雷雨"，使人警醒。这样写雨景，其实也表达了诗人对人生的体验。第六行至第十行诗句意境突转，使前五行诗成为铺垫。诗人"最爱"的还是那将雨未雨的"天"，"虽然是灰色的却透明"，"它蕴着一种无声的期待"，并会有"清脆的鸟啼"式的意外之喜。原来，诗人不但欣赏现实生活中已经呈现的美，更喜欢那期待之中的美好憧憬。鸟啼声提升了全诗意境，将自然美与人情美融成了一片。

这首诗在艺术上没有刻意追求韵脚的整齐，而是采用了无韵的自由诗体，看起来字数大体相当，体现了新月派诗人注重的建筑美。诗中借鉴了传统诗歌的创作手法，注重意境的营造。

译诗力争再现各种雨景和意境，有一定韵律和节奏。

34. 雨巷

戴望舒

撑着油纸伞,独自彷徨在
悠长、悠长又寂寥的雨巷,
我希望逢着一个丁香一样地
结着愁怨的姑娘。

她是有丁香一样的颜色,
丁香一样的芬芳,
丁香一样的忧愁,
在雨中哀怨,哀怨又彷徨;

她彷徨在这寂寥的雨巷,
撑着油纸伞像我一样,
像我一样地默默彳亍着,
冷漠,凄清,又惆怅。

她默默地走近,走近,
又投出太息一般的眼光,
她飘过,像梦一般地,
像梦一般地凄婉迷茫。

像梦中飘过一枝丁香地,
我身旁飘过这个女郎;
她静默地远了,远了,

到了颓圮的篱墙,
走尽这雨巷。

在雨的哀曲里,消了她的颜色,
散了她的芬芳,消散了,
甚至她的太息般的眼光,
丁香般的惆怅。

撑着油纸伞,独自彷徨在
悠长、悠长又寂寥的雨巷,
我希望飘过一个丁香一样的
结着愁怨的姑娘。

34. An Alley in the Rain

By Dai Wangshu

Holding an oil-paper umbrella, I wander alone
A long, long, solitary alley in the rain,
Hoping to chance upon a lilac-like
Melancholy girl.

She is the color of lilac,
Fragrant as lilac,
Melancholy as lilac,
Plaintive and tentative in the rain.

She wanders in the solitary alley in the rain,

Holding an oil-paper umbrella,

And strolling in silence just like me,

Aloof, forlorn, and melancholy.

She silently walks closer, closer,

Casting a glance of sign,

And floats by like a dream

In melancholy confusion.

Like a lilac floating by in dream,

The girl floats past me;

Quietly she pads away and away

To a solitary wall,

Disappearing in the alley of rain.

In the mournful song of the rain, her color fades,

Her fragrance faints,

So do her glance of sign

And lilac-like melancholy.

Holding an oil-paper umbrella, I wander alone

A long, long, solitary alley in the rain,

Hoping to chance upon a lilac-like

Melancholy girl.

译后小记

《雨巷》是中国诗人戴望舒(1905—1950)于1927年创作的一首现代诗。诗题译为"*An Alley in the Rain*",没有选择"lane",因为"alley"更像"小巷","lane"更像是"小径"。(Alley is a narrow street with walls on both sides; Lane is a narrow way or road.)

《雨巷》中,诗人用象征性的意象及意象群来营建抒情空间,传达内心情感,这就在选词措字上给翻译提出了要求,如:"寂寥的雨巷","a solitary alley";"逢着","chance upon";"哀怨又彷徨","plaintive and tentative";"冷漠,凄清,又惆怅","aloof, forlorn, and melancholy";"太息般的眼光","glance of sign";等等。笔者在翻译时努力寻找丁香般忧郁的词汇。

35. 蛇

冯至

我的寂寞是一条长蛇，
冰冷地没有言语——
姑娘，你万一梦到它时
千万啊，莫要悚惧！

它是我忠诚的侣伴，
心里害着热烈的乡思；
它在想那茂密的草原，——
你头上的，浓郁的乌丝。

它月光一般轻轻地，
从你那儿潜潜走过；
为我把你的梦境衔下来，
像一只绯红的花朵！

35. *Snake*

By Feng Zhi

My loneliness is a long snake,
Cold and silent —
Lass, if by chance you dream about it

Anyway, don't be scared of it!

It is my faithful companion
With a strong nostalgia in its heart;
It yearns for the lush grassland —
On your head, the thick black hair.

Gentle as the moonlight,
It sneaks past you;
Taking away your dream for me,
Like a scarlet flower!

译后小记

　　诗人选取"蛇"这一冰冷不语的意象隐喻"我"相思的寂寞、热烈、苦闷、期盼等错综的情感和情绪。既有中国古典诗歌的优美意境，又创造性地在表现手法上融合了象征派诗歌的一些要素，使此诗饱含着象征性和诗意。此诗有着无限的解读，故直译之，追求自然流畅、清新自然，不作过多的阐释。

36. 我是一条小河

冯至

我是一条小河,
我无心由你的身边绕过
你无心把你彩霞般的影儿
投入了我软软的柔波。

我流过一座森林,
柔波便荡荡地
把那些碧翠的叶影儿
裁剪成你的裙裳。

我流过一座花丛,
柔波便粼粼地
把那些凄艳的花影儿
编织成你的花冠。

无奈呀,我终于流入了,
流入那无情的大海
海上的风又厉,浪又狂,
吹折了花冠,击碎了裙裳!

我也随了海潮漂漾,
漂漾到无边的地方
你那彩霞般的影儿
也和幻散了的彩霞一样!

36. *I Am a River*

By Feng Zhi

I am a river
Flowing by you unintentionally,
You throw your rosy shadow unintentionally
Into my soft ripples.

I flow through a forest;
The soft ripples swing
Cut out the shadows of the green leaves
Into your skirt.

I flow by a clump of flowers,
The soft ripples shimmering
Wave the delicate flowers
Into your corolla.

Whatever, I finally flow
Into the merciless sea;
The wind is strong, the waves wild,
Which blow the corolla, break the skirt!

I floated with the tides too,
Floating to infinity;
Your rosy shadow
Disappears illusively as the rosy clouds!

译后小记

《我是一条小河》是现代诗人冯至(1905—1993)于1925年创作的一首诗,此诗采用以人拟物的手法,把人比作小河,然后以其流过森林、流过花丛和流入大海的途程为抒情线索,委婉地表达了诗人对恋人一往情深的怀念和不可改易的情谊,于哀愁中见执著。

在翻译时,笔者注重语义的连贯、语篇的流畅和情感的真挚。

37. 我们有时度过一个亲密的夜

冯至

我们有时度过一个亲密的夜，
在一间生疏的房里，它白昼时
是什么模样，我们都无从认识，
更不必说它的过去未来。原野——
一望无边地在我们窗外展开，
我们只依稀地记得在黄昏时
来的道路，便算是对它的认识，
明天走后，我们也不再回来。
闭上眼吧！让那些亲密的夜
和生疏的地方织在我们心里：
我们的生命像那窗外的原野，
我们在朦胧的原野上认出来
一棵树、一闪湖光、它一望无际
藏着忘却的过去、隐约的将来。

37. Sometimes We Spend an Intimate Night

By Feng Zhi

Sometimes we spend an intimate night
In a strange room. What it looks like
By day time, We never know,

Not to mention its past and future. The field —
Is spreading outside our Windows.
We remember only dimly at dusk
The way of coming, kind of recognition of it.
We will never come back after we leave tomorrow.
Close your eyes! Let those intimate nights
And strange places weave in our hearts:
Our lives are like the fields outside the window.
We recognized in the hazy plain
A tree, a flash of lake light. It is boundless
Hiding the forgotten past and the vague future.

译后小记

《我们有时度过一个亲密的夜》是现代诗人冯至（1905—1993年）创作的一首十四行诗，为一种引进的西方格律诗歌形式。其结构"有起有落，有张有弛，有期待有回答，形势错综而又整齐，韵法穿来穿去"，其容量表达了一段完整的事件和思想，诗歌在起、承、转、合中有着反复变化的韵，起着引导情感又平衡情感、节制情感的作用，将诗人主观的感受和体验升华为客观的理性。

诗意就在字里行间，按原诗译出即可，译诗没有作过多调整。

38. 我爱这土地

艾青

假如我是一只鸟,
我也应该用嘶哑的喉咙歌唱:
这被暴风雨所打击着的土地,
这永远汹涌着我们的悲愤的河流,
这无止息地吹刮着的激怒的风,
和那来自林间的无比温柔的黎明……
——然后我死了,
连羽毛也腐烂在土地里面。

为什么我的眼里常含泪水?
因为我对这土地爱得深沉……

38. *I Love This Land*

By Ai Ching

If I were a bird,
I shall also sing with a hoarse throat:
For the land that was whipped by the storm,
For the river that is forever surging our anger and grief,
For the frenzied wind blowing endlessly,
And for the soft dawn light through the woods…

—And then I shall die,
Even my feathers shall rot in the soil.

Why do I always have tears in my eyes?
Cause I love this land deeply all my life…

译后小记

《我爱这土地》是现代诗人艾青于1938年写的一首现代诗。这首诗以"假如"领起，用"嘶哑"形容鸟儿的歌喉，接着续写出歌唱的内容，并由生前的歌唱，转写鸟儿死后魂归大地，最后转由鸟的形象代之以诗人的自身形象，直抒胸臆，托出了诗人那颗真挚、炽热的爱国之心。

译诗采用虚拟语气，按原诗节奏深情译出。

39. 一朵野花

陈梦家

一朵野花在荒原里开了又落了，
不想到这小生命，向着太阳发笑，
上帝给他的聪明他自己知道，
他的欢喜，他的诗，在风前轻摇。

一朵野花在荒原里开了又落了，
他看见青天，看不见自己的渺小，
听惯风的温柔，听惯风的怒号，
就连他自己的梦也容易忘掉。

39. *A Wild Flower*

By Cheng Mengjia

Blooms and blasts in the field a wild flower;
Unexpected, to the sun smiles the little power.
God has endowed him wisdom he knows;
His happiness, his poem in the wind blows.

Blooms and blasts in the field a wild flower;
He sees the sky but not his own little power.
Getting used to the gentle wind, the howl wind,
Even his own dreams are gone with the wind.

译后小记

此诗写了一朵野花的自然、自在、自信的纯美，并以优美的笔调歌咏它，蕴含乐观、昂扬、超脱的生命态度与情趣。全诗形式整齐，通篇押韵，和谐流畅，是标准的新月格律诗，落笔舒缓有致，情绪自然朴素，咏物以喻人。

译诗第一节的第一句为"A wild flower blooms and blasts in the field"的倒装，"blooms and blasts"（开花和枯萎），押头韵；第二句也是倒装句，"unexpected"是形容词作评注性状语，完整的句子为"The little power smiles to the sun，(which is) unexpected"；第三句的"给"译为"endow"（赋予；使天生拥有）。第二节的第三句"Getting used to…"为现在分词短语表原因。

40. 冬夜

穆旦

更声仿佛带来了夜的严肃,
寂寞笼罩在墙上凝静着的影子,
默然对着面前的一本书,疲倦了
树,也许正在凛风中瑟缩,

夜,不知在什么时候现出了死静,
风沙在院子里卷起来了;
脑中模糊地映过一片阴暗的往事,
远处,有凄恻而尖锐的叫卖声。

40. *A Winter Night*

By Mu Dan

The night-clock seems striking the solemn of night;
Loneliness envelops the silent shadow on the wall;
I stare at an open book blankly; tired and tall
Are trees, maybe, huddling in the wintry wind tight.

The night, before I know, has become dead still;
The wind rolls up the dust in the yard wild.
A dim vision of the past flashes across my mind;
In the distance, a cry of a peddler, sad and shrill.

译后小记

原诗注重意境和节奏，译诗再现作者所听、所见、所感、所想，注重再现原诗意境和意象，并采用抱韵 abbacddc。

"更声……带来了……严肃"译为"The night-clock … struck the solemn"，后查到《德伯家的苔丝》中有："The clock struck the solemn hour of one…""默然对着面前的一本书"中的"默然"理解为"茫然地""呆呆地"，作者心意已不在书本之间，故译为"blankly"；第五行的"still"为"悄悄地""静静地"，与"unknowingly"相呼应，意为"不知不觉之间"；"风沙在院子里卷起来了"，实则卷起的应是尘土，故译"沙"为"dust"；"bygone"指过去的(不愉快的)事。

41. 云

穆旦

凝结在天边,在山顶,在草原,
幻想的船,西风爱你来自远方,
一团一团像我们的心绪,你移去
在无岸的海上,触没于柔和的太阳。

是暴风雨的种子,自由的家乡,
低视一切你就洒遍在泥土里,
然而常常向着更高处飞扬,
随着风,不留一点泪湿的痕迹。

41. *Clouds*

By Mu Dan

You gather on horizon, on top of mountains, on prairie.
Fantasy ship, west wind loves you from afar.
Mass by mass like our minds, you drift away
Upon the boundless sea, and disappear by touch of the soft sun.

You are the seeds of the storm, the hometown of freedom.
Looking down on everything, you spread yourself in the soil;
But usually you fly higher and higher
Along with the wind, leaving no trace of tears.

译后小记

《云》一诗两节，运用比喻和拟人来写云，"幻想的船""一团一团的心绪""暴风雨的种子""自由的家乡"，云的姿态变幻，观云者的遐想，全都跃然纸上。此诗翻译几乎是一次完成，有两点经验分享：一是汉语的无主句，如第一二节首句的主语为题目的"云"，翻译时采用第二人称"you：译出；二是第二节第二行的"泥土"译为"soil"（土地、土壤），不宜译为"dirt"（污泥）。

42. 远和近

顾城

你，
一会儿看我，
一会儿看云。

我觉得，
你看我时很远，
你看云时很近。

42. *Distant and Close*

By Gu Cheng

You
Now look at me,
Now look at the clouds.

I feel
You are distant when you look at me,
Yet close when you look at the clouds.

译后小记

《远和近》是顾城的名作。这首诗看似短小平常，却是发前人所未发，以极简之诗句发出极深之哲思，通过云和我的焦点转换，远和近的空间距离对比，折射出心理距离的远和近。恰到好处的留白手法，给这首小诗以强大生命力和无尽的阐释空间。

诗题"远和近"，既指物理空间的远和近，也指心理空间的远和近，考虑到这两个维度，英译为"distant and close"，而不译为"far and near"，或"far or near"。

第一节，"一会儿……一会儿……"表示"时不时"的意思，而不是"一段时间"，译为"now...now..."，不译为 for a while。

原诗注重意境，话到即止，译诗也不作过多阐释。

43. 微微的希望

顾城

我和无数
不能孵化的卵石
垒在一起

蓝色的河溪爬来
把我们吞没
又悄悄吐出

没有别的
只希望草能够延长
它的影子

43. A Glimmer of Hope

By Gu Cheng

I stay together

With countless pebbles

That do not hatch

The blue river creeps up

Engulfs us

And then exhales us

There is no choice
But to hope the grass extending
Its shadow

译后小记

现代诗不求押韵，但有其自然节奏，如同呼吸一样，翻译此诗，笔者主要追求语义流畅，节奏自然，注重选词措字。

"微微的希望"就是"一丝希望"，故译为"a glimmer of hope"。

第一节，英汉语序不同，有所调整；很容易出现汉语思维，将"不能"译为"cannot"；笔者将"不能孵化的卵石"译为"pebbles that do not hatch"。

第二节，译好三个动词"爬""吞""吐"是关键，译者选择有拟人化的三个动词"creep""engulf""exhale"来译。

第三节，译者采用了一个存在句"There is no choice but to hope…"来译。"能够"一词同样不必译为"can"之类，"but"之后相当于紧接一个名词短语。

44. 门前

顾城

我多么希望,有一个门口

早晨,阳光照在草上

我们站着

扶着自己的门扇

门很低,但太阳是明亮的

草在结它的种子

风在摇它的叶子

我们站着,不说话

就十分美好

有门,不用开开

是我们的,就十分美好

早晨,黑夜还要流浪

我们把六弦琴交给他

我们不走了

我们需要土地

需要永不毁灭的土地

我们要乘着它

度过一生

土地是粗糙的,有时狭隘

然而,它有历史

有一份天空,一份月亮

一份露水和早晨

我们爱土地

我们站着

用木鞋挖着泥土

门也晒热了

我们轻轻靠着，十分美好

墙后的草

不会再长大了

它只用指尖，触了触阳光

44. *On the Doorstep*

By Gu Cheng

How I wish, to be on the doorstep

In the morning, the sun shines on the grass

We stand

Leaning on the door

The low door, but it is sunny

The grass is seeding

The wind is shaking leaves

We stood quiet, without a word

It is just fine

There is a door, but we don't have to open it

It's ours which is fine

In the morning, the night is still wandering

We give him a guitar

We're not leaving

We need a land

A land never to be destroyed

We're going to ride on it

The whole life

The land is rough and sometimes narrow

However, it has a history

It has a part of sky, a part of moon

A portion of dew and morning

We love the land

We stand

Digging up the soil with wooden shoes

The door is getting hot

We lean against each other, and it's fine

The grass behind the wall

Never grows up again

It simply touches the sunlight with the tips of its fingers

译后小记

《门前》文字浅近，描绘了诗人与恋人依偎门窗前，阳光温和，风摇草结的一幅图景，写出了"家"的温馨，流露出诗人对农耕文明的留恋，对朴实田园生活的向往。

翻译时为了保留诗中的这份宁静与美好，译者注意选词措字。如："家门口"，"on my doorstep"；"扶着自己的门扇"，"lean on or against the door"；"草在结它的种子/风在摇它的叶子"，这里"它的"不必译出，如"The grass is seeding / The wind is shaking leaves"；"我们站着，不说话"是为突出彼此的默契，译为"We stood quiet, without a word"；诗中"乘着"是"依靠"之意，正好与"ride on"一致。

译诗中多跨行诗句。

45. 错误

郑愁予

我打江南走过
那等在季节里的容颜如莲花的开落

东风不来，三月的柳絮不飞
你的心如小小的寂寞的城
恰若青石的街道向晚
跫音不响，三月的春帷不揭
你的心是小小的窗扉紧掩

我达达的马蹄是美丽的错误
我不是归人，是个过客……

45. *A Mistake*

By Zheng Chouyu

As I pass through Jiangnan
The face waiting in the season flowers and fades as a waterlily

The catkins will not flutter in spring until the vernal breeze arrives
Your heart is a little town so lonesome
As the street of bluestone slab when twilight drawing on

The spring curtain will not lift before the echo of footsteps
Your heart is a little window closed tight.

Clop-clop, the sound of my horse-hoofs is a beautiful mistake
I'm not homecoming but just passing through…

译后小记

"失落"在江南烟水中，等一个人，那期待的容颜如莲花般美丽，可是，终究不是归人，容颜如莲花凋零。思念、等待，最是伤人。

"我达达的马蹄"是个美丽的错误，诗文也阐释了诗题"错误"，故"错误"在诗题和诗中应译为单数名词"a mistake"。

中文是意合的语言，本来少用连词，诗歌更是如此，而翻译为英语，需要逻辑关联词交代句子间的逻辑关系，如第一节，译者加了"as"；再如第二节的"until""so…as""when""before"；第三节的"but"。

46. 她那颗小小的心

俞大纲

那一晚，天黑，也没有星，
我和她，数着成串的街灯，
我们并肩走去，一盏，两盏，三盏，……
看不分明，也数不清，
我说"别再数，这没意思的街灯，
我有一盏，明亮，活跳，永远照着我，
那就是你——你那颗小小的心。"

这一晚，天黑，也没有星，
我和她，又来到街灯下步行，
头上照着，一盏，两盏，三盏，……
我们不再数，也数不清，
四周像死去，没有声音，
这下我听见自己说话的灵魂，
他说"今天，你该知道，照着你，
只有街灯，可怕的年月，
淹没她那颗小小的心，
你别傻，谁还肯给你一点光明。"

46. *Her Little Heart*

By Yu Dagang

That night, dark and starless,
She and I count the strings of street lamps;

We walked together, one, two, three…
We can't see it, nor count it,
I said, "stop counting those boring street lights.
I have a light, bright, alive, shining on me forever;
That's you — your little heart."

This night, dark and starless,
She and I walk again under the lamp;
There are lamps over head, one, two, three…
We don't count anymore; we can't count anymore.
It is a deafening silence around, without a sound.
Now I hear my soul speak,
"Well," he says, "you should know only the streetlights
Shine on you; the terrible years
Has drowned her little heart;
Don't be silly; who will give you a little light."

译后小记

这首诗选自《新月诗选》，诗中充满意象。第一小节，诗人将"她小小的心"比作照亮自己的最明亮的"街灯"；第二小节，"街灯"明亮，可是岁月淹没了"她小小的心"，不再给诗人以光明。

47. 从前慢

木心

记得早先少年时
大家诚诚恳恳
说一句　是一句

清早上火车站
长街黑暗无行人
卖豆浆的小店冒着热气

从前的日色变得慢
车，马，邮件都慢
一生只够爱一个人

从前的锁也好看
钥匙精美有样子
你锁了　人家就懂了

47. *Old Days Slow*

By Muxin

I remember old teen days
We were sincere I'd say
Every word it weighs

Train station in early morning

The long street dark and empty

The little soybean milk shop was steaming

The sun used to be slow

The car, horse, and mail slow too

Life was only enough to love one so

The old lock was nice to eye

The key was in delicate style

Once you locked, others wouldn't try

译后小记

木心先生这首诗，语言浸着"五四"新文学的滋味，意象透着"从前"词与物的美，这慢里透着的人性朴素、浪漫、耐性、果决，而且是让人看得懂却深觉文学的魅力。最难译的是那慢里透着的意与味。译者尽量以同样的慢节奏再现原诗"意味"，英译诗歌每行的音节数与原文相当，行尾保留一定音韵效果，每节押韵 aba。

48. 秋

海子

秋天深了，神的家中鹰在集合
神的故乡鹰在言语
秋天深了，王在写诗
在这个世界上秋天深了
得到的尚未得到
该丧失的早已丧失

48. *Autumn*

By Haizi

Deep autumn, under the roof of God
Eagles are gathering, talking
Deep autumn, King is writing a poem
Autumn is deep in the world
Those supposed to get haven't got yet
Those supposed to leave have already left

译后小记

这首诗短小而意味深长，前两句呈现一个动态画面及背景，即在深秋神的家里，鹰在集合，鹰在言语；第三句是一幅静态画面；后三句表达诗人在秋天的寂寞与失落，富含哲理。

49. 面朝大海,春暖花开

海子

从明天起,做一个幸福的人
喂马,劈柴,周游世界
从明天起,关心粮食和蔬菜
我有一所房子,面朝大海,春暖花开

从明天起,和每一个亲人通信
告诉他们我的幸福
那幸福的闪电告诉我的
我将告诉每一个人

给每一条河每一座山取一个温暖的名字
陌生人,我也为你祝福
愿你有一个灿烂的前程
愿你有情人终成眷属
愿你在尘世获得幸福
我只愿面朝大海,春暖花开

49. *A Promising Life*

By Haizi

From tomorrow on, I'll be a happy guy
Feeding horses, chopping wood, travelling around the world

From tomorrow on, I'll care about grains and greens
I'd have a house facing the sea with spring flowers

From tomorrow on, I'll write to each of my relatives
I'll tell them my happiness
What the lightning of happiness has inspired me
I'll tell everyone

I'll give each river and each mountain a warm name
Bro, I also bless you
Wish you have a bright future
May you lovers tie the knot
May you be happy forever
I only wish to live in a house facing the sea with spring flowers

译后小记

此诗是诗人写于1989年1月13日的一首抒情诗，距诗人在同年3月卧轨自杀只有两个多月的时间。诗人将直抒胸臆与暗示、象征手法结合起来，全诗清澈又深厚，明朗又含蓄，畅快又凝重，抒发了诗人对幸福的向往和内心的孤独凄凉。

汉语重意象，英语重具象。翻译时，不可简单直译。诗题"面朝大海，春暖花开"是诗人向往的幸福生活，如果直译成"facing the sea with spring flowers"，则不能明白其中的逻辑关系，笔者根据全诗意境，意译为"a promising life"，意为诗人的理想生活。

汉语省略主语，英语须补充。这首诗的第一节，全部是述说"我"；而第二节和第三节，也就是第二部分，全部是述说"我和他人"。在译诗中，根据需要，添加了多个主语"I"。汉语多用动词，英语多用名词。如"喂马，劈柴，周游世界"，译者采用动名词形式表达。

译诗注意措辞，如"粮食和蔬菜"，译者没有译为"food and vegetables"，而是译为"grains and greens"，因为后者有头韵效果；"告诉"一词，译者根据逻辑主语不同分别选择了"tell""inspire"。"陌生人"，译者不译为"stranger"，一是因为这不是一个称呼用词，二是因为"stranger"是一个没有温度的词，诗人送去的祝福是很温暖的，不能跟在一个没有温暖的称呼之后。译者采用了一个口语化的对陌生人的友好称呼"bro"来译，以增强祝福画面的真实感。祝福之后的三个"愿……"是祝福的内容，这里须注意语义连贯。

50. 九月

海子

目击众神死亡的草原上野花一片
远在远方的风比远方更远
我的琴声呜咽　泪水全无
我把这远方的远归还草原
一个叫马头　一个叫马尾
我的琴声呜咽 泪水全无

远方只有在死亡中凝聚野花一片
明月如镜高悬草原映照千年岁月
我的琴声呜咽　泪水全无
只身打马过草原

50. *Lunar September*

By Haizi

The prairie witnessed the death of pantheon presents boundless wild flowers

The wind afar is even farther away from afar

My strings sob with tearless grief

I return to the prairie the afar from afar

One is called horse-head, the other horse-tail

My strings sob with tearless grief

The afar only in death converges a sheet of wild flowers

The mirror-like moon hangs high over the land reflecting time of thousands of years

My strings sob with tearless grief

Alone I ride a horse across the prairie

译后小记

这首诗歌极其沉痛，充满神秘氛围，渺远的时间与旷阔的空间扭结纠缠在一起，生命与死亡在互相诠释，翻译就是体验和再现诗人所感所想。诗人借助"草原""野花""秋风""马头琴""明月"等意象，营造旷远深邃的悲秋寂寥，故将"九月"译为"Lunar September"，因为农历的九月有更多的文化遐想。翻译时坚持"译意不译字"，如"我的琴声呜咽"，译为"My strings sob"（我的琴呜咽）；"泪水全无"，不译为"without tears"，而译为"with tearless grief"（欲哭无泪的悲伤）。

第二部分
英语诗歌汉译

Part II
English-Chinese
Poetry Translation

51. Since Brass, Nor Stone, Nor Earth, Nor Boundless Sea

By William Shakespeare

Since brass, nor stone, nor earth, nor boundless sea
But sad mortality o'er-sways their power,
How with this rage shall beauty hold a plea,
Whose action is no stronger than a flower?
O, how shall summer's honey breath hold out
Against the wrackful siege of batt'ring days,
When rocks impregnable are not so stout,
Nor gates of steel so strong, but time decays?
O fearful meditation! where, alack,
Shall time's best jewel from time's chest lie hid?
Or what strong hand can hold his swift foot back?
Or who his spoil of beauty can forbid?
  O, none, unless this miracle have might,
  That in black ink my love may still shine bright.

51. 金铜、岩石、大地或海洋

威廉·莎士比亚

金铜、岩石、大地或海洋,
没有不屈服于那凄惨的无常,
美,她的生命力不比花朵旺,

纵然愤怒，怎敌那肃杀苍茫？
　　啊，夏日溢流香，怎能抵抗
　　朝风暮雨，岁月流逝无光芒。
　　岩墙钢门看似坚固，并不强，
　　它们迟迟早早都要败给时光。
　　啊，哪，呜呼！骇人的冥想！
　　珍宝能否免于收进时光宝箱？
　　或有力的手阻止他步履匆忙？
　　抑或谁能制止他把美丽夺抢？
　　　　啊，没有谁，除非奇迹力量，
　　　　唯吾爱隽永诗墨，留光遗香。

译后小记

　　威廉·莎士比亚（William Shakespeare，1564年4月23日—1616年4月23日），华人社会常尊称为莎翁，是英国文学史上最杰出的戏剧家，也是欧洲文艺复兴时期最重要、最伟大的作家，当时人文主义文学的集大成者，以及全世界最卓越的文学家。莎士比亚流传下来的作品包括37部戏剧、154首十四行诗、两首长叙事诗。

　　16世纪初，十四行诗体传到英国，风行一时，到16世纪末，十四行诗已成为英国最流行的诗歌体裁，产生了锡德尼、斯宾塞等著名的十四行诗人。其后，英国戏剧家、诗人莎士比亚发展了这种诗体，称之为"莎士比亚体"或"伊丽莎白体"，由三节四行诗和两行对句组成，其押韵格式为 abab cdcd efef gg，每行诗句有十个抑扬格音节。

　　此诗为莎士比亚体十四行诗的第六十五首，主题还是爱情，译诗有一定音韵节奏，一韵到底。

52. When, in Disgrace with Fortune and Men's Eyes

By William Shakespeare

When, in disgrace with fortune and men's eyes
I all alone beweep my outcast state,
And trouble deaf heaven with my bootless cries,
And look upon myself, and curse my fate,
Wishing me like to one more rich in hope,
Featured like him, like him with friends possessed,
Desiring this man's art, and that man's scope,
With what I most enjoy contented least;
Yet in these thoughts myself almost despising,
Haply I think on thee, and then my state,
Like to the lark at break of day arising
From sullen earth, sings hymns at heaven's gate;
 For thy sweet love remembered such wealth brings
 That then I scorn to change my state with kings.

52. 时运不济遭贬谤

威廉·莎士比亚

时运不济遭贬谤
独自哭泣心凄凉

振聋发聩徒悲伤

顾影自怜詈命相

前途似锦尤企望

一如他风流倜傥

多才多艺见识广

心底渴望余惆怅

汲汲所欲心鄙夷

所幸忆君神飞起

云雀高飞破晓时

天门高唱赞美诗

　君之情谊真财富

　纵然王位懒回顾

译后小记

　　莎士比亚的十四行诗从第十八首到第一百二十六首是写给一个贵族男青年的，该青年相貌俊美，诗人主要歌颂他的美貌及与他的友谊。第二十九首就是其中的一首。这首诗热情地歌颂爱情，诗人在创作这首诗时，充分发挥了十四行诗的长处，采用了"先抑后扬"手法，层层推进，波澜起伏，道出了诗人思想感情的发展变化。全诗总体是五音步抑扬格，但第十一行多一个音节，最后一个音节"-sing"又是轻音节，与第九行的"-sing"押阴性韵——押韵的音节后还有一个相同的轻读音节。另外，此行中的轻读和重读音节安排有变化，第一个音步（"like to"）变为扬抑格，从而使前两个音步（"like to / the lark"）构成"重-轻-轻-重"的模式，把两个轻音节连在一起，给人以云雀飞翔的迅速感。而最后的"arising"又构成"轻-重-轻"的模式，又给人以云雀在空中上下飞翔的升降感。这行诗被誉为声音与意义巧妙结合的成功范例。末行

"state"有双关意思，一是与第十行的"state"（心境）相联系，二是在"to change my state with kings"一语中又有"throne"的意思。

诗人在诗中把"爱"视为珍宝，给人一种鼓舞奋发的力量。如前所述，采取"先抑后扬"的手法。头四句感叹自身生不逢时。接下来的四句自惭形秽，怨天尤人，痛苦万状。最后六句，笔锋一转，表露他对"爱情"的珍视。爱的魅力使他忘记一切，丢掉过去，立即满心高兴地像云雀一样飞腾天空，翱翔欢唱。尤其是"所幸忆君神飞起"这一句表达了诗人对"爱"的态度，视"爱"为珍宝。这种"先抑后扬"的笔法，层层推进，波澜起伏，饶有兴趣。

译诗紧跟原诗，以顿代步，有一定韵律和节奏，行尾押韵 aaaa aaaa bbbb cc。

53. *Farewell Sweet Grove*

By George Wither

Farewell!

Sweet groves, to you!

You hills, that highest dwell;

And all you humble vales, adieu!

You wanton brooks, and solitary rocks,

My dear companions all! And you, my tender flocks!

Farewell my pipe, and all those pleasing songs, whose moving strains

Delighted once the fairest nymphs that dance upon the plains!

You discontents, whose deep and over-deadly smart

Have, without pity, broke the truest heart.

Sighs, tears, and every sad annoy,

That erst did with me dwell,

And all other joys,

Farewell!

53. 再见，美丽树林

乔治·威瑟

再见

美丽树林

再见高高山峦

低低山谷幽幽树荫
奔腾的小溪静默的岩床
亲爱的小伙伴和温顺的羔羊
再见芦笛愉悦的歌声动人的旋律
美丽的仙子曾随之草原翩翩起舞
你的不悦过于深沉过于精明
不懂怜惜伤了真诚的心
叹息眼泪烦恼悲伤
往昔一切如烟
所有欢畅
再见

译后小记

乔治·威瑟(George Wither，1588—1667)，英国诗人，推崇"为艺术而艺术"的唯美主义、形式主义和后现代主义。

此诗以奇特的菱形构建全诗，匠心独特，可谓"形美感目"。全诗14行，每行音节分别为 2-4-6-8-10-12-14-14-12-10-9-6-5-2，音节数的逐行变化，形成诗歌独特的形貌。原诗行尾押韵 abab ccddee fafa，可谓"音美感耳"。此诗为"菱形挽歌"，告别树林、山岚、小溪、岩石、朋友、羊群、往昔的欢愉与悲伤，可谓"意美感人"。

译诗14行，每行字数为 2-4-6-8-10-12-14-12-10-8-6-4-2，字数的逐行变化，构成完美菱形诗。译诗，必须传承原诗诗意，这一点，译诗也还是紧贴原诗。译诗押尾韵 abab ccddee fafa，只是原诗行尾押完全韵，译诗个别为邻通押韵，如"明"与"心"。

翻译难得完美，译者就是在"音美""形美""意美"之间，寻求一个最佳平衡点。

54. *To Celia*

By Ben Jonson

Drink to me only with thine eyes,
And I will pledge with mine;
Or leave a kiss in the cup
And I'll not look for wine.
The thirst that from the soul doth rise
Doth ask a drink divine;
But might I of Jove's nectar sup,
I would not change for thine.

I sent thee late a rosy wreath,
Not so much honouring thee
As giving it a hope that there
It could not withered be;
But thou thereon didst only breathe
And sent'st it back to me;
Since when it grows, and smells, I swear,
Not of itself but thee!

54. 致西莉亚

本·琼森

惊鸿一瞥吾心醉
连忙凝眸紧相随

酒樽残留一香吻
吾将不再饮甘醇
灵魂深处饥渴滋
祈求上天遗恩赐
纵使琼浆玉液淳
不与他人换酒樽

吾将玫瑰赠送卿
此意非是表尊敬
唯有希望在其间
玫瑰不枯常鲜妍
卿只一闻花气息
玫瑰遂回我手里
从此花香远益清
不似玫瑰恰似卿

译后小记

本·琼森(Ben Jonson，约1572年6月11日—1637年8月6日)，英格兰文艺复兴时期剧作家、诗人和演员。

此诗刻画了一位陷入爱情无法自拔的男子。诗歌语言朴素，富有音乐美。诗中用了许多古香古色的词，如"thine""doth"等，还用了一些典故，如Jove(罗马神话中的主神)、Nectar(希腊神话中众神所饮的酒)等，再次赋予诗歌古典色彩。诗歌中的意象鲜明，涉及眼睛、酒樽、美酒、玫瑰花环等。

全诗共分两节，每节八行，格律不太明显，但韵式明显，每节又有两个相同的韵式：abcbabcb。

译诗贴近原诗诗意，每行三顿，并取汉诗"三字尾"的形式，行尾押韵，格式为aabbccbb　aabbccaa。

55. *To Blossoms*

By Robert Herrick

Fair pledges of a fruitful tree,
  Why do ye fall so fast?
    Your date is not so past,
But you may stay yet here awhile
  To blush and gently smile,
    And go at last.

What, were ye born to be
  An hour or half's delight,
    And so to bid good-night?
'Twas pity Nature brought ye forth
  Merely to show your worth,
    And lose you quite.

But you are lovely leaves, where we
  May read how soon things have
    Their end, though ne'er so brave:
And after they have shown their pride
  Like you, awhile, they glide
    Into the grave.

55. 花儿

罗伯特·赫里克

花儿许下满树硕果，
　缘何如此匆匆？
　　尚在约期之中，
实可再作片刻逗留，
　羞红笑靥温柔，
　　消逝影踪。

为何，此生前来
　只为片刻欣喜，
　　然后挥手致意？
可惜，上苍让你问世，
　利用你的价值，
　　随之抛弃。

然而经由美丽花瓣，
　读懂好景不长，
　　尽管不曾刚强：
如同你们傲娇一番，
　短暂停留，悄然
　　滑入坟场。

译后小记

读罢 *To Blossoms*，是否想起曹雪芹笔下的《葬花吟》呢？花儿凋残，漫天旋转，世间美好却不长久，心中难免一声声哀叹。这首诗格律工整，三节六行，其韵式也较规律，分别为 abbccb、addeed 和 affggf，属于混用的韵式。译文韵式为 aaabbb、cddddd 和 effggg。特别值得一提的是，诗中第三节第一行"leaves"一词，在这里与"blossom"词汇连贯，意为"花瓣"。雪莱的诗 *Music When Soft Voices Die* 中有一句："Rose leaves, when the rose is dead, /Are heaped for the beloved's bed."这里的"rose leaves"也是玫瑰花瓣。

56. *To a Young Lady*

By William Cowper

Sweet stream, that winds through yonder glade,
Apt emblem of a virtuous maid—
Silent and chaste she steals along,
Far from the world's gay busy throng;
With gentle yet prevailing force,
Intent upon her destined course;
Graceful and useful all she does,
Blessing and blest where'er she goes;
Pure-bosom'd as that watery glass,
And Heaven reflected in her face.

56. 致佳人

威廉·柯柏

清清小溪，蜿蜒林间，
恰似佳人，纯真甘甜——
沉静圣洁，脚步悄悄，
远离尘世，纷繁喧嚣；
动作轻盈，力量持久，
执着前路，永不回头；
举止优雅，千古流芳，

所到之处，福泽绵长；

心若明镜，透若冰霜，

悠悠天堂，映在脸庞。

译后小记

威廉·柯珀（William Cowper，1731—1800），另翻译为威廉·考珀、威廉·古柏，英国现代派诗人。他在清纯的自然诗歌描写中融入了人物性格的刻画，其诗作深切动人。有人将此诗诗题译为"*A Comparison, To a Young Lady*"，是用林间溪流比喻一个品德贤良，清雅脱俗，低调然而富有个性的女性，故可把诗的题目翻译成"致佳人"或"比照：致佳人"。

全诗十行，每行八到九个音节，采用联韵。此诗翻译经验概括起来为：语篇连贯，解读诗意；行尾联韵，再现诗韵；以逗代步，重构节奏；隐喻修辞，放空想象。

57. Eternity

By William Blake

He who binds to himself a joy
Does the winged life destroy
He who kisses the joy as it flies
Lives in eternity's sunrise

57. 永恒

威廉·布莱克

译文一：

沉浸欢愉不自知
必断生存之羽翅
吻别快乐任其飞
沐浴永恒之晨曦

译文二：

生于安乐兮
折尔之羽翼
挥手自兹去
永沐于晨曦

译后小记

威廉·布莱克(William Blake,1757—1827),英国第一位重要的浪漫主义诗人、版画家,英国文学史上最重要的伟大诗人之一,虔诚的基督教徒。主要诗作有诗集《纯真之歌》《经验之歌》等。

原诗四行两句,调整自然语序为:"He who binds to himself a joy does destroy the winged life; He who kisses the joy as it flies lives in eternity's sunrise."这是一首跨行诗,押韵 aabb,译诗有七言和五言两个版本,采取东方韵 aaba。

58. *The Reverie of Poor Susan*

By William Wordsworth

At the corner of Wood Street, when day light appears,

Hangs a Thrush that sings loud, it has sung for three years:

Poor Susan has passed by the spot, and has heard

In the silence of morning the song of the Bird.

'Tis a note of enchantment; what ails her? She sees

A mountain ascending, a vision of trees;

Bright volumes of vapour through Lothbury glide,

And a river flows on through the vale of Cheapside.

Green pastures she views in the midst of the dale,

Down which she so often has tripped with her pail;

And a single small cottage, a nest like a dove's,

The one only dwelling on earth that she loves.

She looks, and her heart is in heaven: but they fade,

The mist and the river, the hill and the shade:

The stream will not flow, and the hill will not rise,

And the colours have all passed away from her eyes!

58. 苏珊幻梦

威廉·华兹华斯

伍德街角，晨曦初现，
画眉高唱，婉转三年；
可怜苏珊，途经此地，
鸟鸣悦耳，四周沉寂。

歌声迷醉，心意朦胧：
山峦起伏，树木葱茏；
青山苍翠，薄雾缥缈，
潺潺溪涧，淙淙欢跳。

青青牧场，谷间盘绕，
手提小桶，蹦跳奔跑；
农舍一间，鸽巢小屋，
栖身此窝，心意知足。

内观一切，恍若天堂！
云河迷雾，渐入苍茫；
溪水不流，山岚不起，
眼前景色，褪色消失！

译后小记

威廉·华兹华斯(William Wordsworth，1770—1850)，英国浪漫主义诗人。

此诗中的"poor"并非"贫穷的"，因为诗文并不谈"贫与富"，而是表达诗人对于 Susan 的情感态度，接近"可怜的""不幸的"之意，这与诗文中体现的一致，诗题中的"poor"可省略不译。其次，专有名词"Wood Street"，音译为"伍德街"。"Lothbury"和"Cheapside"则略去不译。

诗中通过对苏珊梦幻的描写，展现她对故乡和田园生活的眷恋和向往。诗人以此表达了自己厌倦城市生活的心情和态度。这首诗以抑扬格为主旋律写成，每行四个音步，读起来有舒缓轻松的感觉，从而使梦幻色彩在不紧不慢的气氛中得以铺展，加强了如梦似幻的效果。原诗韵式为 aabb ccdd eeff gghh，译文遵从同样韵式，以逗代步，每行八字四逗，节奏与原诗一致。

59. *The Lost Love*

By William Wordsworth

She dwelt among the untrodden ways
Beside the springs of Dove;
A maid whom there were none to praise,
And very few to love:

A violet by a mossy stone,
Half hidden from the eye!
—Fair as a star, when only one
Is shining in the sky.

She lived unknown, and few could know
When Lucy ceased to be;
But she is in her grave, and oh,
The difference to me!

59. 失落的爱

威廉·华兹华斯

栖居荒凉
鸽子泉旁；
无人赞扬，

无人爱慕的姑娘：

青苔石旁紫罗兰，
隐约入眼帘！
——靓丽如孤星，
天空值此耀眼睛。

露西生前无人识，
不知何时无声息；
她在坟冢里，
噢！与我阴阳相异！

译后小记

威廉·华兹华斯(William Wordsworth，1770—1850)，英国浪漫主义诗人，曾为桂冠诗人。其诗歌理论动摇了英国古典主义诗学的统治，有力地推动了英国诗歌的革新和浪漫主义运动的发展。他是文艺复兴运动以来最重要的英语诗人之一，其诗句"朴素生活，高尚思考"(plain living and high thinking)被作为牛津大学基布尔学院的格言。

The Lost Love 诗句朴素，情感至深，比喻恰如其分。译诗三节，共12行，隔行押完全韵，即 abab cdcd efef。译诗押尾韵 aaaa bbcc dddd，力求留住诗义与诗意。

60. *Lines Written in Early Spring*

By William Wordsworth

I heard a thousand blended notes,
    While in a grove I sat reclined,
In that sweet mood when pleasant thoughts
    Bring sad thoughts to the mind

To her fair works did Nature link
    The human soul that through me ran;
And much it grieved my heart to think
    What man has made of man.

Through primrose tufts, in that green bower
    The periwinkle trail'd its wreaths;
And'tis my faith that every flower
    Enjoys the air it breathes.

The birds around me hopp'd and play'd,
    Their thoughts I cannot measure—
But the least motion which they made,
    It seem'd a thrill of pleasure.

The budding twigs spread out their fan
    To catch the breezy air;
And I must think, do all I can,
    That there was pleasure there.

If this belief from heaven be sent,
　　If such be Nature's holy plan,
Have I not reason to lament
　　What man has made of man?

60. 早春随笔

威廉·华兹华斯

斜倚小树独坐林间
　　聆听协奏音符万千
心情沉静愉悦无比
　　一缕忧思骤起

自然造物巧夺天工
　　与我人类灵魂相通
不禁心头忧思悲戚
　　人类为何如此

报春花丛中绿荫处
　　长春藤拖曳花环簇
每朵花我确信不疑
　　惬意呼吸空气

周遭鸟儿蹦跳嬉戏
　　他们所想令我迷离
只是动作纵然微小
　　透着兴奋美好

嫩枝丫舒展小叶扇
　　微风轻抚绚烂
尽我所能，不由得想
　　那里幸福徜徉

倘若此念上天授意
　　倘若此想自然设计
我怎么能不悲不叹
　　人类为何这般

译后小记

　　此诗描写了诗人坐在树荫下享受大自然美景的情景。林间一切如此和谐，花儿，鸟儿，叶儿都在享受大自然的清新和欢快，触景伤怀。从万物的欢乐中，华兹华斯想到了人间的痛苦和悲伤。人本为大自然的一部分，理应加入大自然欢乐的海洋，但是人间的情况却不是如此，是人类自身造成了人间的痛苦和悲伤。诗歌含蓄地表达了作者对世间不平的抗议和对公平社会的渴望。令诗人伤感的却是人类不能和大自然万物一样和谐共存。

　　原诗每行8个音节或6个音节，主旋律为四音步抑扬格，每节押韵格式为abab，节奏感很强，但时有变调，很好地契合了诗人起伏的思绪。笔者翻译时，主要是紧贴诗人的思想情绪，力求流畅自然，真实再现原诗的诗意与诗义，译诗每行8字或6字，译诗每节押韵格式为aabb。

61. *The Daffodils*

By William Wordsworth

I wandered lonely as a cloud
That floats on high o'er vales and hills,
When all at once I saw a crowd,
A host, of golden daffodils,
Beside the lake, beneath the trees,
Fluttering and dancing in the breeze.

Continuous as the stars that shine
And twinkle on the milky way,
They stretched in never-ending line
Along the margin of a bay:
Ten thousand saw I at a glance
Tossing their heads in sprightly dance.

The waves beside them danced, but they
Out-did the sparkling waves in glee:
A Poet could not but be gay
In such a jocund company!
I gazed—and gazed—but little thought
What wealth the show to me had brought;

For oft, when on my couch I lie
In vacant or in pensive mood,

They flash upon that inward eye
Which is the bliss of solitude;
And then my heart with pleasure fills
And dances with the daffodils.

61. 水仙花

威廉·华兹华斯

独自漫游，我似浮云
飘过山岗，荡过山村
倏然之间，连绵无边
金黄水仙，映入眼帘
青青湖畔，绿茵树下
翩翩起舞，馥郁典雅

连绵成片，绚烂若星
遍布银河，闪亮晶莹
蜿蜒湖湾，绵延数里
蓓蕾初绽，亭亭玉立
一目千株，目不暇接
吐花展瓣，随风摇曳

清波碧浪，竞相起舞
花姿娇媚，自叹不如
凌波仙子，花黄叶翠

诗人骚客，莫不陶醉
凝视良久，心无旁骛
眼前此景，竟是财富

此后常常，沙发静躺
恬淡虚无，沉思冥想
水仙浮现，绿草如茵
心境空灵，天赐福音
悠然我心，愉悦沉静
水仙弄舞，曼妙轻盈

译后小记

William Wordsworth（华兹华斯），英国18世纪浪漫主义诗人的代表之一，又称"湖畔诗人"。此诗共分四节，一节六行，每行八个音节，主旋律为抑扬格四音步，每节押韵格式相同，都为ababcc。文辞平白易懂，以水仙为题，表达了诗人对自然的热爱，歌颂自然界事物之间的和谐，歌颂自然界与诗人本人之间的和谐。

译诗依照原诗格律，以顿代步，每行八字四顿，行尾押韵aabbcc。

诗歌的翻译不仅是语言的转换，更是一种认知体验，如果执念于字面，容易翻译僵化。如第一节"float"一词，本意"飘荡"，译者分开"飘过""荡过"来译；再如"a crowd""a host"，如果照字面译成"一群群""一簇簇"（水仙花），是否有点别扭，失去诗意；"beside the lake, beneath the trees"如译为"在湖边，在树下"也没什么不对，终归是容易诗意失落。

再如第四节，原诗充满禅意，如不能很好领悟，翻译更是容易流于字面而诗意全无。

值得注意的是，此诗前三节为一般过去时，第四节为一般现在时，前三节是"我似浮云独自漫游偶遇水仙花"的回顾，第四节是水仙花给"我"带来的精神财富的具体呈现，翻译时，译者加了"此后常常"来区分。

62. *Desideria*

By William Wordsworth

Surprised by joy—impatient as the Wind
I turn'd to share the transport—O with whom
But Thee, deep buried in the silent tomb,
That spot which no vicissitude can find?
Love, faithful love, recall'd thee to my mind—
But how could I forget thee? Through what power,
Even for the least division of an hour,
Have I been so beguiled as to be blind
To my most grievous loss? —That thought's return
Was the worst pang that sorrow ever bore,
Save one, one only, when I stood forlorn,
Knowing my heart's best treasure was no more;
That neither present time, nor years unborn
Could to my sight that heavenly face restore.

62. 渴慕怀旧

威廉·华兹华斯

欣喜若狂——迫不及待,
我欲分享——呜呼!舍你
其谁,深居墓穴沉寂,

那里没有沧桑悲哀？

爱，挚爱，想起你神态——

怎能忘怀？即使假如，

哪怕只是片刻须臾，

我心蒙蔽抛却脑外

心中痛楚？——这一念想

是悲伤之极的苦痛，

只有一人，当我绝望，

懂我心中宝藏已空；

现在抑或将来时光，

眼前再无神圣面容。

译后小记

从语义连贯来理解原诗。"诗人"欣喜若狂，急于与人分享，却发现伊人已然不再，心中感慨万千，于是追思缅怀。

诗题"desideria"是拉丁语，是"desiderium"的复数形式，名词，意为"（如对失去的东西的）渴望，渴求，患失感，怀旧感"，中文没有对应词，试译为"渴慕怀旧"。

从语篇语义连贯来看"transport"与"joy"是同义复现，查辞典"transport"有义项："a state of being carried away by overwhelming emotion"，即狂喜。

此诗中的跨行诗句，加大了理解难度；在翻译时，译者紧贴原诗，基本按照原诗结构来译。如第二行和第三行"O with whom / But Thee"，笔者译为"呜呼！舍你/其谁"。

"Through...Have I been so beguiled as to be blind / To my most grievous loss?"这是一个反问句，表达非常肯定的意思，而不是疑问句。

原诗是韵式规范的十四行诗，首行的"wind"与"find""mind""blind"等古英语押韵，都是/aɪd/，现称作视韵(目韵)；原诗每行十个音节，主旋律为抑扬格四音步，行尾押韵 abba acca dede de；译者紧贴原诗来译，译诗每行八字，行尾同样押韵 abba acca dede de。

63. *My Heart Leaps up When I Behold*

By William Wordsworth

My Heart leaps up when I behold
A rainbow in the sky:
So was it when my life began,
So is it now I am a man,
So be it when I shall grow old,
Or let me die!
The Child is father of the Man:
And I could wish my days to be
Bound each to each by natural piety.

63. 凝眸，我心雀跃

威廉·华兹华斯

天空挂彩虹
我心荡神驰
如是自孩童
成年亦相同
耄耋若非此
毋宁早超脱
三岁看八十
倏然一生过
天性自然通

译后小记

这是一首很短小的哲理诗——时光荏苒,不变的是纯净的心,在自然的护佑下,成人的世界也可以永葆纯真。中国有句俗话,"三岁定八岁,八岁定终身",也有"三岁看八十"的说法,颇有道理。人与人生来秉性不同,人生有几个转折点,但骨子里的东西不会变。

译诗尽量保持"音美、形美、意美",原诗押韵 abccabcde,译诗押韵 abaabcbca。

64. *Hunting Song*

By Sir Walter Scott

Waken, lords and ladies gay!
On the mountain dawns the day;
All the jolly chase is here
With hawk and horse and hunting-spear;
Hounds are in their couples yelling,
Hawks are whistling, horns are knelling,
Merrily, merrily mingle they,
"Waken, lords and ladies gay!"

Waken, lords and ladies gay,
The mist has left the mountain grey;
Springlets in the dawn are steaming,
Diamonds on the brake are gleaming;
And foresters have busy been
To track the buck in thicket green;
Now we come to chant our lay,
"Waken, lords and adies gay!"

Waken, lords and ladies gay!
To the greenwood haste away;
We can show you where he lies,
Fleet of foot and tall of size;
We can show the marks he made

When 'gainst the oak his antlers fray'd;
You shall see him brought to bay,
"Waken, lords and ladies gay!"

Louder, louder chant the lay,
Waken, lords and ladies gay!
Tell them youth and mirth and glee
Run a course as well as we;
Time, stern huntsman! who can balk,
Staunch as hound and fleet as hawk;
Think of this, and rise with day,
Gentle lords and ladies gay!

64. 狩猎歌

沃尔特·司各特

醒醒，老爷太太，好热闹！
山顶微明，天已破晓；
飞鹰跑马，手握猎枪，
欢乐追逐，齐齐亮相；
猎犬双双，叫喊不停，
猎鹰吹哨，号角低鸣，
欢呼欢笑，齐聚一道，
"醒醒，老爷太太，好热闹！"

醒醒，老爷太太，好热闹！
山色空濛，薄雾缥缈；
清晨小溪，雾气腾腾，
草叶钻石，闪亮晶莹；
护林队员，正在忙碌，
绿林丛中，追踪雄鹿；
吟唱歌谣，现在正好，
"醒醒，老爷太太，好热闹！"

醒醒，老爷太太，好热闹
那片绿林，匆匆小跑；
我们知道，他藏在哪，
健步如飞，身形高大；
角撞橡树，磨破橡皮，
我们展示，他的踪迹；
看他被围，无处可逃，
"醒醒，老爷太太，好热闹！"

高声，高声，吟唱歌谣，
醒醒，老爷太太，好热闹！
告诉人们，青春畅欢，
犹如人生，一去无返；
时机，猎人！谁能犹豫，
犬般坚定，鹰般迅速；
想到这儿，与日同高，
温婉老爷太太，好热闹！

译后小记

沃尔特·司各特（Walter Scott，1771—1832），英国诗人和小说家。翻译此诗时，笔者从语篇连贯视角来解读 Hunting Song，重构连贯的中译诗篇，有以下几个翻译难点。

1. 反复重复的一个词"gay"，从语篇语义连贯来看，原诗有条欢快的主线："gay…jolly…merrily…gay；gay…chant our lay…gay；gay…gay；chant the lay…gay…mirth and glee…gay。""gay"与下文狩猎的场面"欢快""热闹"气氛连贯一致；故笔者将"gay"译为"好热闹"，似乎更符合原诗歌情景语境中女仆说话的口吻，俨然清晰可见女仆脸上说起狩猎场面的兴奋表情。

2. 从词语同现关系来看，第二节"The mist has left the mountain grey"中"mist"与"grey mountain"同现于原诗，"mist"是"grey mountain"的逻辑原因，意思是"雾使山变成了灰色"。"grey mountain"不是山的原本面貌，山原本应是青山（green mountain），如果"left"表示"mist""离开""mountain"之意，那么薄雾散去之后的山应该是"green mountain"，而不是"grey mountain"；换言之，与"The mist has left"（薄雾散去）同现的应该是"green mountain"，故笔者译诗中这句为"山色空濛，薄雾缥缈"。这一翻译也契合原诗的时间顺序和情景语境，并与接下来的一句"Springlets in the dawn are steaming"中所描述的"雾气腾腾"连贯一致。

3. 第二节第四行"Diamonds on the brake are gleaming"中的"brake"一词，从语篇连贯看来，与"brake"同现的词有"mountain"（山）、"springlets"（泉）、"forest"（林）等，但"马车""香车"与"山""泉""林"没有同现关系；换言之"马车""香车"不大可能出现在山野之中。因此，笔者大胆猜测"brake"为山中植物，以"brake+植物"在网上搜索到"fern brake"（蕨，羊齿丛），以"fern brake +图片"在网上还可搜索到这一山野植物的图片，这一词义正好符合语境；而上面的

153

"diamonds"指的是"露珠",正好与清晨的"mountain"(山)、"springlets"(泉)、"forest"(林)构成同现关系。

英语格律诗不一定是完全规范的××格×音步,但是主流格律应该突出。《狩猎歌》的主流格律是扬抑格四音步,偶有变化。拙译基本上采用二字顿,以顿代步试图还原原诗节奏。原诗一诗四节,押韵格式为aabbccaa,译诗与原诗音韵节奏一致。

65. *Love's Philosophy*

By Percy Bysshe Shelley

The fountains mingle with the river
  And the rivers with the ocean,
The winds of heaven mix for ever
  With a sweet emotion;
Nothing in the world is single;
  All things by a law divine
In one spirit meet and mingle.
  Why not I with thine? —

See the mountains kiss high heaven
  And the waves clasp one another;
No sister-flower would be forgiven
  If it disdained its brother;
And the sunlight clasps the earth
  And the moonbeams kiss the sea:
What is all this sweet work worth
  If thou kiss not me?

65. 爱的哲学

珀西·比希·雪莱

山泉与溪流相通,
  江河与海洋相融。

风儿碧空唱随从，
　　情深深你侬我侬。
寰宇无物影只单，
　　神赐天条法自然。
世间万物皆连理，
　　为何唯独我和你？

高山与长空吻拥，
　　波浪与波浪交融。
雌雄花蕊情不浓，
　　云失衣裳花失容。
阳光依偎大地欢，
　　月光亲吻深海酣。
一切甜蜜何裨益，
　　倘若你我不亲昵？

译后小记

珀西·比希·雪莱(Percy Bysshe Shelley，1792—1822)，英国著名作家、浪漫主义诗人，被认为是历史上最出色的英语诗人之一。

韵式异化处理：原诗韵式是 ababcdcd；译诗的押韵方式为 aaaabbcc。原诗押完全韵，第一节押的"river"和"ever"，第二节押的"heaven"和"forgiven"，是轻读音节押韵。译诗也有押非完全韵的地方，如第二节的第五句和第六句末的"欢"和"酣"，是邻韵通押。

节奏明快：原诗以抑扬格为主，变格多而灵活，节奏明快，每行三音步或两音步。译文每句七言，步其主要节奏，作三顿步，也求节奏明快。

66. *The Owl and the Pussy Cat*

By Edward Lear

The Owl and the Pussy Cat went to sea

In a beautiful pea-green boat,

They took some honey, and plenty of money

Wrapped up in a five-pound note.

The Owl looked up to the stars above,

And sang to a small guitar,

"O lovely Pussy, O Pussy, my love,

What a beautiful Pussy you are,

You are,

You are!

What a beautiful Pussy you are!"

Pussy said to the Owl, "You elegant fowl!

How charmingly sweet you sing!

O let us be married! Too long we have tarried,

But what shall we do for a ring?"

They sailed away, for a year and a day,

To the land where the Bong-tree grows

And there in a wood a Piggy-wig stood

With a ring at the end of his nose,

His nose,

His nose,

With a ring at the end of his nose.

"Dear Pig, are you willing to sell for one shilling

Your ring?" Said the Piggy, "I will."
So they took it away, and were married next day
By the Turkey who lives on the hill.
They dined on mince, and slices of quince,
Which they ate with a runcible spoon;
And hand in hand, on the edge of the sand,
They danced by the light of the moon,
The moon,
The moon,
They danced by the light of the moon.

66. 猫头鹰和小猫咪

爱德华·李尔

猫头鹰小猫咪出海扬帆，
驾驶一艘豆青色靓小船；
带了蜂蜜还有好多钱币，
包裹在一张五镑纸币里。
猫头鹰仰望天空的星星，
边弹小吉他边唱得动情：
"喔，猫咪！可爱的猫咪，
美丽绝伦的猫咪就是你，
就是你，
就是你！
美丽绝伦的猫咪就是你！"

"优雅的飞禽，"猫咪笑云，

"你的歌声多么甜蜜动人

喔，让我们结婚，结婚！

但我们的戒指在哪儿呢？"

他们继续远航一年又一天，

来到一个地方，长满大树，

树林里站着头蓬乱的小猪。

一枚戒指就在它鼻尖上！

在它鼻尖上，

在它鼻尖上，

一枚戒指就在它鼻尖上！

"小猪啊，愿意一先令交换

戒指？"小猪点头，"愿意。"

拿了戒指，第二天便在一起，

住在山里的火鸡为他们证婚。

他们吃着肉馅啊，肉片，

凭借着锋利的三齿叉匙。

手拉手，他们在沙滩边，

一起欢快舞蹈在月光下，

月光下，

月光下，

一起欢快舞蹈在月光下！

译后小记

爱德华·李尔（Edward Lear，1812—1888）的打油诗 *The Owl and the Pussy Cat*，或者说"谐趣诗"（nonsense poetry），读起来朗朗上口。

李尔在写这些诗歌的时候,把音乐美放在很高的位置。有些词甚至听起来很融洽,但是并没有确切的含义。比如"runcible"这个词,就是作者自己造出来好玩的。再如"They dined on mince, and slices of quince",这里"quince"(温柏,温柏树)完全是为了和"mince"(肉馅)押韵。

翻译此诗,除了语义一致外,音韵节奏也非常重要,译诗基本上每行四顿,行尾押韵,读起来有点像儿歌。

67. The Night Has a Thousand Eyes

By Francis William Bourdillon

The night has a thousand eyes,
And the day but one;
Yet the light of a bright world dies
With the dying sun

The mind has a thousand eyes,
And the heart but one;
Yet the light of a whole life dies
When love is done.

67. 黑夜有一千只眼睛

弗朗西斯科·威廉·鲍迪伦

黑夜有一千只眼睛,
白昼只有一只;
然光明世界之光明
随日落而消逝。

头脑有一千只眼睛,
心灵只有一只;
然整个生命之光明
随情尽而消失。

译后小记

Francis William Bourdillon（1852—1921）的这首诗简洁易懂，两节诗行结构相似，是一首跨行诗，押韵格式为 abab。译诗保持同样的语言风格，只在个别用词有变化，如"die"在第一节译为"消逝"，第二节译为"消失"。

68. *On the Sale by Auction of Keats' Love Letters*

By Oscar Wilde

These are the letters which Endymion wrote
  To one he loved in secret, and apart.
  And now the brawlers of the auction mart
Bargain and bid for each poor blotted note,
Ay! For each separate pulse of passion quote
  The merchant's price. I think they love not art
  Who break the crystal of a poet's heart
That small and sickly eyes may glare and gloat.

Is it not said that many years ago,
  In a far Eastern town, some soldiers ran
  With torches through the midnight, and began
To wrangel for mean raiment, and to throw
  Dice for the garments of a wretched man,
Not knowing the God's wonder, or His woe?

68. 济慈情书被拍卖有感

奥斯卡·王尔德

这些书信出自恩底弥翁笔下,
  写给曾经暗恋却已分手对象。

　　　　拍卖市场现正叫嚣吵吵嚷嚷，
　　为字迹斑驳的信笺讨价还价。
　　唉！诗人每一次激情的脉搏
　　　　都明码标价。艺术无所谓，
　　　　他们将诗人的玻璃心击碎，
　　病态小眼睛发着光幸灾乐祸。

　　是否曾经听说，多年以前，
　　　　远东小镇，一些士兵出逃。
　　　　他们手持火把彻夜通宵
　　争抢几件衣裳不惜翻脸；
　　　　抛掷骰子只为一件长袍，
　　不知上帝诧异，伤心难言？

译后小记

　　奥斯卡·王尔德（Oscar Wilde，1854—1900），出生于爱尔兰都柏林，19世纪英国（准确来讲是爱尔兰，但是当时由英国统治）最伟大的作家与艺术家之一，以剧作、诗歌、童话和小说闻名，唯美主义代表人物，19世纪80年代美学运动的主力和90年代颓废派运动的先驱。

　　彼特拉克的十四行诗形式整齐，音韵优美，以歌颂爱情，表现人文主义思想为主要内容。每首诗分成两部分：前一部分由两段四行诗组成，后一部分由两段三行诗组成，即按四、四、三、三编排。其押韵格式为 abba abba cde cde 或 abba abba cdc dcd 以及 abba abba cdc cdc 等格式，前八行称为吻韵，亦称抱韵，后六行韵式称为联韵；每行诗句十一个音节，通常用抑扬格。十四行诗形象生动，结构巧妙，音乐性强，起承转合自如。一般在前八句叙述事情，提出问题，表现情绪。

后六句回答、解决问题，缓和情绪，由最后的对句概括内容、点明主题。其题材除了爱情之外，还可扩及政治、宗教或个人领域。

奥斯卡·王尔德的这首十四行诗，押韵格式为 abba abba cdd cdc，译诗步原韵。

69. On the Hill-Side

By Radclyffe Hall

A Memory

You lay so still in the sunshine,
So still in that hot sweet hour—
That the timid things of the forest land
Came close; A butterfly lit on your hand,
Mistaking it for a flower.

You scarcely breathed in your slumber,
So dreamless it was, so deep—
While the warm air stirred in my veins like wine,
The air that had blown through a jasmine vine,
But you slept—and I let you sleep.

69. 山坡上

雷克里夫·霍尔

一抹回忆

你静静地躺在阳光下
那么安谧，在那热辣甜蜜时刻——

林间胆小精灵
悄悄走近，蝴蝶翩跹于你手心
以为那是花朵

安睡中你如此恬淡
虚无，沉静——
暖风如酒在我血管里流动
那暖风也曾拂过茉莉花藤
而你睡着了——我任由你恬睡

译后小记

诗人以细腻的笔触记下恋人们在山坡上恬静美好的瞬间。

70. *Leisure*

By W. H. Davies

What is this life if, full of care,
We have no time to stand and stare.

No time to stand beneath the boughs,
And stare as long as sheep or cows.

No time to see, when woods we pass,
Where squirrels hide their nuts in grass.

No time to see, in broad daylight,
Streams full of stars, like skies at night.

No time to turn at Beauty's glance,
And watch her feet, how they can dance.

No time to wait till her mouth can
Enrich that smile her eyes began.

A poor life this if, full of care,
We have no time to stand and stare.

70. 闲暇

威廉·亨利·戴维斯

什么生活，满腹闷愁，
没有闲暇停留凝眸；

没有闲暇树下悠悠，
任性凝眸犹如羊牛；

没有闲暇，林间逗留，
察松鼠藏果草里头；

没有闲暇，晴日闲赏，
溪流闪烁，夜空星光；

无暇侧目美人回眸，
观其玉足，蹁跹自由；

无暇等待朱唇微启
荡漾眼角微微笑意；

什么生活，满腹闷愁，
没有闲暇停留凝眸。

译后小记

这是英国诗人威廉·亨利·戴维斯(W. H. Davies)的一首风格清新、自然质朴的小诗,诗人提醒人们留出片刻闲暇静赏生活中的美,其背后蕴藏着对生活的哲思,特别适合对当下提出的慢生活。原诗主旋律为四音步抑扬格,采用联韵 aa bb cc dd ee ff aa,译文以顿代步,一行四逗,同样采用联韵,押韵格式为 aa aa aa bb aa cc aa,译文第一节和最后一节构成回环修辞。

71. *Remember Me When I Am Gone Away*

By Christina Georgina Rossetti

Remember me when I am gone away,

Gone far away into the silent land;

When you can no more hold me by the hand,

Nor I half turn to go, yet turning stay.

Remember me when no more day by day

You tell me of our future that you plann'd

Only remember me; you understand

It will be late to counsel then or pray

Yet if you should forget me for a while

And afterwards remember, do not grieve;

For if the darkness and corruption leave

A vestige of the thoughts that once I had,

Better by far you should forget and smile

Than that you should remember and be sad.

71. 请勿忘我,当我离开

克里丝蒂娜·乔治娜·罗塞蒂

请勿忘我,当我离开,

前往远方,幽静所在;

再也不能,你拽我手,

片刻犹豫，欲去还留。
请勿忘我，不如往昔，
听你描绘，未来日子，
唯我不忘；你心了然，
劝告祈祷，为时已晚。
片刻须臾，将我暂忘，
复上心头，莫要悲伤。
黑暗降临，肉体消失，
若存一念，泉下有知，
毋宁忘却，内心欢喜，
尤胜思念，忧伤悲戚。

译后小记

这是克里丝蒂娜·乔治娜·罗塞蒂（Chiristina Georgina Rossetti）的抒情诗代表作。克里丝蒂娜·乔治娜·罗塞蒂是但丁·迦百列·罗塞蒂的妹妹，也是先拉斐尔派诗人。她的诗受其兄影响，兼有抒情性和神秘性，并带有悲哀和象征的色彩。但与其兄相比又各有特色：哥哥的诗浓艳华丽，而妹妹的诗哀婉朴素，哥哥重感官而妹妹重虔信。

这首十四行诗，为五音步抑扬格，行尾押韵 abba abba cdd ece，译诗以顿代步，每行八字四顿，行尾押韵 aabb ccdd ee cccc。

72. *What Is Poetry?*

By Eleanor Farjeon

What is Poetry? Who knows?
Not a rose, but the scent of the rose;
Not the sky, but the light in the sky;
Not the fly, but the gleam of the fly;
Not the sea, but the sound of the sea;
Not myself, but what makes me
See, hear, and feel something that prose
Cannot: and what it is, who knows?

72. 何为诗

埃莉诺·法杰恩

何为诗,孰知之乎?
非玫瑰,乃其香也,
非天空,乃其光也,
非萤虫,乃其亮也,
非大海,乃其声也。
非吾身,乃触吾心,
感吾耳目,而散文之不能也,
何为诗,孰知之乎?

译后小记

埃莉诺·法杰恩(1881—1965),英国作家,著有儿童故事、戏剧、诗歌、传记、历史和讽刺作品。

辞典上对 poetry 的释义有二:

①(作为文学形式的)诗,诗歌,韵文。(Poems, considered as a form of literature, are referred to as poetry.)

②诗的意境;诗一般美的事物。(You can describe something very beautiful as poetry.)

原诗读来,笔者理解诗人笔下的"poetry"不是作为文学形式的"诗",而是诗之所以为"诗"的"诗意"。原诗八行,行尾押完全韵,押韵格式为 aa bb cc aa,且首尾呼应。翻译时,我们也只能传递其诗义和诗意,没能押韵。

73. *When You Are Old*

By William Butler Yeats

When you are old and grey and full of sleep,
And nodding by the fire, take down this book,
And slowly read, and dream of the soft look
Your eyes had once, and of their shadows deep;

How many loved your moments of glad grace,
And loved your beauty with love false or true,
But one man loved the pilgrim Soul in you
And loved the sorrows of your changing face;

And bending down beside the glowing bars,
Murmur, a little sadly, how Love fled
And paced upon the mountains overhead
And hid his face amid a crowd of stars.

73. 当你老了

威廉·巴特勒·叶芝

当你老了，头发花白睡意沉，
炉边打盹，就请取下这诗歌，
慢慢品读，想你眼神多柔和，

多么温存，瞳影深邃忒迷人；

曾经多人，爱恋你青春时光，
赞你美貌，抑或真心或假情，
独有一人，钟情你圣洁魂灵，
怜你脸上，岁月沧桑独怅惘；

弯腰躬身，斜倚炉旁暗伤神，
喃喃低语，哀叹爱神不眷顾，
遁入无形，群山之巅缓踱步，
浩瀚繁星，隐匿脸庞不留痕。

译后小记

威廉·巴特勒·叶芝，爱尔兰诗人、剧作家，1923 年诺贝尔文学奖获得者，"爱尔兰文艺复兴运动"的领袖。诗人艾略特曾盛赞叶芝是"当代最伟大的诗人"，而我更喜欢同为诗人的奥登为叶芝写的悼词——"疯狂的爱尔兰将你刺伤成诗"。

《当你老了》是叶芝于 1893 年创作的一首诗歌，是叶芝献给友人茅德·冈热烈而真挚的爱情诗篇。诗歌语言简明，但情感丰富真切。诗人采用了多种艺术表现手法。文章通过深入剖析诗作中诗人所使用的艺术表现手法，诸如假设想象、对比反衬、意象强调、象征升华，再现了诗人对茅德·冈忠贞不渝的爱恋之情，揭示了现实中的爱情和理想中的爱情之间不可弥合的距离。

全诗主旋律是抑扬格五音步，如首行："When you/ are old/ and grey/ and full/ of sleep。"（下画线音节重读，为"扬"，余为"抑"）抑扬格是英语口语的自然节奏，通常有一种沉思之感，正好体现诗人沉思怀旧之情。拙译试用以顿代步的方法,用每行五个顿步对应原诗的五个音步。

原诗每节均用抱韵(又名吻韵)押韵格式为 abba。其浪漫韵名,也正好寓意诗人对茅德·冈眷恋不变之情。拙译步其韵式,以期保留作者赋诗的初衷。

74. A Dream Within a Dream

By Edgar Allan Poe

Take this kiss upon the brow!
And, in parting from you now,
Thus much let me avow —
You are not wrong, who deem
That my days have been a dream;
Yet if hope has flown away
In a night, or in a day,
In a vision, or in none,
Is it therefore the less gone?
All that we see or seem
Is but a dream within a dream.

I stand amid the roar
Of a surf-tormented shore,
And I hold within my hand
Grains of the golden sand —
How few! Yet how they creep
Through my fingers to the deep,
While I weep — while I weep!
O God! Can I not grasp
Them with a tighter clasp?
O God! Can I not save
One from the pitiless wave?

Is all that we see or seem

But a dream within a dream?

74. 梦中之梦

埃德加·爱伦·坡

请带走眉间这吻！
在你我分手时分，
到此我得承认——
没错，如你认定
我本从来都是梦；
然若希望已溜边
在夜晚抑或白天，
梦幻与虚无之间，
因此就无以为失？
一切我们所见似见
不过一场梦，梦中之梦。

我站在海边，
浪花肆卷，波涛怒号，
我攥紧手里，
金沙一粒粒——
寥寥可数！可它们仍旧溜走，
悄悄钻过我的指头，
无语凝噎——无语凝噎！

哦，上帝啊！难道我不能

将这沙粒儿攥得更紧？

哦，上帝啊！难道我不可

于这无情波涛中拯救一颗？

难道一切我们所见似见

不过一场梦，梦中梦？

译后小记

埃德加·爱伦·坡（Edgar Allan Poe）（1809—1849），19世纪美国诗人、小说家和文学评论家，美国浪漫主义思潮时期的重要成员。

第一节的首句"Take this kiss upon the brow!"是个祈使句，诗人让与之别离的那个人带着眉间的亲吻离开。从第一节可见，诗人自己和对方的情感复杂，分手也许是诗人生活如在梦中，对方生活在现实世界，难以沟通，这也契合了诗人的现实生活情况，生活放荡不羁、潦倒不堪。

第二节，诗人在诗中用手中抓不住的沙子，来比喻人的一生所经历的一切，也都像留不住、握不牢的沙子一样，过眼烟云、稍纵即逝。所以，在中国，文人也常说，"人生如梦""春梦一场"。而爱伦坡则更进一步，说人生是"梦中之梦"，那就更加虚无缥缈、不可捉摸，也无可挽留了！

两节的结尾句基本一样，只是第一节是个陈述句，第二节改成了疑问句。笔者的理解是：第一节，他不但同意对方的断言，说他是一场梦，人生岁月只是一场梦而已。第二节，则是诗人向上帝的祈求。他虽然知道岁月只是春梦一场，但是却希望上帝能让他多多少少挽留一点"希望"，哪怕就像一粒沙子那么渺小的"希望"也好。所以，最后诗人用疑问句来质疑：难道生活真的只是"梦中之梦"吗？

75. *I Hear America Singing*

By Walt Whitman

I Hear America singing, the varied carols I hear,

Those of mechanics, each one singing his, as it should be, blithe and strong,

The carpenter singing his, as he measures his plank or beam,

The mason singing his, as he makes ready for work, or leaves off work,

The boatman singing what belongs to him in his boat, the deck-hand singing on the steamboat deck,

The shoemaker singing as he sits on his bench, the hatter singing as he stands,

The wood-cutter's song, the ploughboy's on his way in the morning, or at noon intermission, or at sundown,

The delicious singing of the mother, or of the young wife at work, or of the girl sewing or washing,

Each singing what belongs to him or her and to none else,

The day what belongs to the day—at night, the party of young fellows, robust, friendly,

Singing, with open mouths, their strong melodious songs.

75. 我听见美利坚在歌唱

沃尔特·惠特曼

我听到美利坚在歌唱，唱着各种各样的歌：

机械师唱着自己的歌，那是欢快而有力的歌；

木匠量木板或房梁，一边唱着他的歌；

泥瓦匠准备工作或离开工作，都唱着歌；

船夫在船上唱着属于他的歌，水手在汽船甲板上唱着歌；

鞋匠坐在凳子上唱歌，做帽子的站着也唱歌；

伐木工的歌，牵耕牛的孩子早晨、午歇、日落也都唱着歌；

母亲或年轻妻子工作时，还有姑娘们在做针线活或洗衣裳时甜美地唱着歌；

每个人都唱着属于自己的歌，而不是别人的歌；

白天唱着白天的歌——夜晚，一群健壮友善的年轻人

放开嗓门唱着他们那雄壮悦耳的歌。

译后小记

沃尔特·惠特曼（Walt Whitman，1819—1892），出生于纽约州长岛，美国著名诗人、人文主义者，创造了诗歌的自由体（Free Verse），其代表作品是诗集《草叶集》（*Leaves of Grass*）。

诗人创造性地运用了富有诗意的"歌唱"和由现在分词构成的排比并列结构，生动传神地把当时美国的勃勃生机展现在读者面前。惠特曼的伟大之处，在于他的作品始终贯穿着人民立场和朴素的唯物史观，这为后世提供了宝贵的精神财富。惠特曼骄傲地宣称，他的诗中没有了"旧世界赞歌中高大突出的人物"，而有的是"作为整个事业及未来主

要成就的最大因素的各地普通农民和机械工人"。从城市到农村，从海上到陆地，整个美利坚人民都在歌唱，他们快乐、幸福、乐观；他们自信、自豪、积极向上、勤奋努力；他们的国家和平安宁、欣欣向荣，充满希望。这就是创造者的"美国梦"。每个劳动者都有属于自己的歌，即每个劳动者在国家的建设中都感到非常重要；每个劳动者都唱着自己的歌参加劳动，每个劳动者都感到幸福快乐。整首诗突出了民主、自由，语言简单，口语化，高昂流畅。

  翻译时，除了追求语义一致外，还保持了明快的节奏。

76. *A Bird Came down the Walk*

By Emily Dickinson

A Bird came down the Walk—
He did not know I saw—
He bit an Angle Worm in halves
And ate the fellow, raw,

And then he drank a Dew
From a convenient Grass—
And then hopped sidewise to the Wall
To let a Beetle pass—

He glanced with rapid eyes
That hurried all around—
They looked like frightened Beads, I thought—
He stirred his Velvet Head

Like one in danger, cautious,
I offered him a Crumb
And he unrolled his feathers
And rowed him softer home—

Than Oars divide the Ocean,
Too silver for a seam—
Or Butterflies, off Banks of Noon
Leap, plashless as they swim.

76. 小鸟沿小径走来

艾米莉·狄金森

小鸟沿小径走来——
不知一旁我在瞧——
他把一条蚯蚓啄开
再吃掉那家伙，生嚼，

他将清露饮吞
取自近旁草叶上——
又侧身跳到旁边墙脚根
来给甲虫把路让——

急促地左顾右盼
他那滴溜溜的眼眸——
活像受惊的珠子，我想——
见他抖了抖毛茸茸的头

好像身处险境，十分小心，
我给他分点碎面包
而他立刻展开羽翎
往回飞去一路轻飘——

胜过船桨划海面，
波光银白水无痕——
胜过蝴蝶，晌午草梗边
跃下，游弋无溅声。

译后小记

艾米莉·狄金森(Emily Dickinson, 1830—1886),美国著名诗人,被誉为"现代主义先驱"。她的诗歌主要写生活情趣、自然、生命等,诗风凝练、比喻新颖,喜用格律、不顾语法,极富独创性。诗人创作了500多首关于生态话题的自然诗歌,体现了诗人强烈的生态意识。诗人追求心灵与大自然的交融,重视寻找与建立人与自然亲近和谐的关系,这契合了现代生态批评理论的思想,体现了一种人类与自然和谐共存的审美诗意。

《小鸟沿小径走来》是一首白描诗,诗人偶遇一只小鸟吃虫,主角是小鸟,"我"是旁观者。狄金森用简洁的笔触勾勒出小鸟的形象,用小鸟怡然自得捕食蚯蚓、饮水、让路等一连串的动作(came down, bit, ate, drank, hopped, glanced, stirred, unrolled, rowed)去塑造自己,而作者却隐蔽起来(I saw, I thought),后来因"我"的介入(I offered)惊扰了小鸟的安宁,结果是小鸟展翅飞走。全诗共分五个诗节,每节四行,抑扬格三音步为主旋律,全诗有一个句号,是一个完整连贯的动画。

翻译此诗有四点心得:译"意"不译"字";跟随标点符号与诗歌节奏;"以顿代步"还原原诗节奏;保持诗韵与诗味,从而做到江枫先生主张的译诗"力求形神皆似,形似而后神似"的诗歌翻译标准。

77. From Blank to Blank

By Emily Dickinson

A Threadless Way
I pushed Mechanic feet—
To stop— or perish— or advance—
Alike indifferent—

If end I gained
It ends beyond
Indefinite disclosed—
I shut my eyes— and groped as well
'Twas lighter— to be Blind

77. 来自虚无　去往虚无

艾米莉·狄金森

一条无痕之路
我拖着机械双脚——
或驻步——或麻木——或前行——
同样漫不经心——

即便到达终点
我发现终点之外

模糊一片——
关闭双眼——摸索向前
更加明亮——倘若看不见

译后小记

原诗第二节，不太好理解。"It ends beyond / Indefinite disclosed—"，这句话的理解要联系上下文，前一句"If end I gained"是虚拟语气，意思为"即便我到了终点"，这一句意思为"(我发现)路终结在一片模糊之处"，也就和下文的"关闭双眼——摸索向前"连贯起来。

译诗和原诗保持同样的节奏，原诗并不押韵，译诗行尾部分押韵。

78. *I Died for Beauty*

By Emily Dickinson

I died for Beauty — but was scarce
Adjusted in the Tomb
When one who died for Truth, was lain
In an adjoining room —

He questioned softly "Why I failed?"
"For Beauty", I replied—
"And I — for Truth —Themselves are One —
We Brethren, are", He said—

And so, as Kinsmen, met a Night—
We talked between the Rooms —
Until the Moss had reached our lips—
And covered up — our names—

78. 我为美而死

艾米莉·狄金森

我为美而死——但几乎不
适应坟墓
这时有人为真理而死,就躺在

隔壁邻间——

他轻声问："我怎么倒下啦？"
"为美"，我答——
"而我——为真理——二者同一——
我们是，兄弟"，他说——

于是，像亲人，相逢黑夜——
我们隔墙交谈——
直到苔藓爬上我们的唇——
覆盖——我们的名字——

译后小记

  艾米莉·狄金森喜欢用标点符号来表达诗歌的节奏，译诗保持标点符号与原诗一致。翻译时选词措字要根据语境来搭配，如第一节"in an adjoining room"（隔壁邻间），第三节"We talked between the Rooms"（隔墙交谈），"room"一词不能死译。

79. *I'm Nobody! Who Are You?*

By Emily Dickinson

I'm Nobody! Who are you?
Are you — Nobody — Too?
Then there's a pair of us!
Don't tell! They'd advertise — you know!

How dreary — to be — Somebody!
How public — like a Frog —
To tell one's name — the livelong June —
To an admiring Bog!

79. 我是无名小辈，你呢？

艾米莉·狄金森

我是无名小辈，你呢？
你——也——没啥辈？
那我们凑一对！
嘘！他们爱宣扬呢——你懂的！

无聊啊——做个——名人！
粉墨登场——像只青蛙——
宣告自己名号——漫长的六月——
对着仰慕的沼泽呱呱！

译后小记

译诗标点与原诗一致,保留与原诗一致的节奏。为突出对话效果,译诗运用了语气助词"呢""啊"之类,并注意说话的口吻。基于译者对原诗的理解和认知,译诗在表达方面也有自己的特色,如"how public"译为"粉墨登场"。

80. *The Soul Selects Her Own Society*

By Emily Dickinson

The Soul selects her own Society—
Then—shuts the Door—
To her divine Majority—
Present no more—

Unmoved—she notes the Chariots—pausing—
At her low Gate—
Unmoved—an Emperor be kneeling—
Upon her Mat—

I've known her—from an ample nation—
Choose One—
Then—close the Valves of her attention—
Like Stone—

80. 灵魂选择自己的伴侣

艾米莉·狄金森

灵魂选定自己的伴侣——
然后——紧闭心门——
她那神圣殿堂——

不再容他人——

不为所动——她注意到高轩——停留——
在她低矮的门前——
不为之所动——她注意到皇帝拜倒——
在她脚下的草垫——

我知道她——自众生芸芸的王国——
选择一个——
然后——关注的阀门紧锁——
心若磐石——

译后小记

译诗语序与原诗相同，标点符号与原诗一致，保留与原诗一致的节奏。

81. *I Took One Draught of Life*

By Emily Dickinson

I took one Draught of Life —
I'll tell you what I paid —
Precisely an existence —
The market price, they said.

They weighed me, Dust by Dust —
They balanced Film with Film,
Then handed me my Being's worth —
A single Dram of Heaven!

81. 我啜饮过生命的琼浆

艾米莉·狄金森

我啜饮过生命的琼浆——
告诉你吧,活脱脱——
为此付出了一世芬芳——
不过市价,他们说。

他们称了称我的分量,分斤掰两——
他们算了算兑换多少,锱铢必较,
然而给了我生命所值价码——
只不过小小一片天堂!

译后小记

"take a draught of"意为"吸了一口",为了诗意,题目译为"我啜饮过生命的琼浆"。

译诗语序基本与原诗相同,标点符号与原诗基本一致,保留与原诗一致的节奏。只有第一节"I'll tell you what I paid — / Precisely an existence — ",因为英语句子中的副词位置比较灵活,翻译时,笔者将"precisely"移到动词之前来译。此诗有不少隐喻,不宜字对字直译。"an existence",译者没有译为"一生",而是译为"一世芬芳",使得第一节行尾押韵 abab,保留原诗意象,留住诗意。

第二节,"weighed""balanced",分别是"称重""兑换";"dust by dust""film with film",译者用"分斤掰两""锱铢必较"来译,显化"他们"的计较,同时,"量"与"两","少"与"较"产生很好的音韵效果。

82. *Wild Nights*

By Emily Dickinson

Wild Nights —Wild Nights!
Were I with thee
Wild Nights should be
Our luxury!

Futile —the Winds —
To a Heart in port —
Done with the Compass —
Done with the Chart!

Rowing in Eden —
Ah, the Sea!
Might I but moor —Tonight —
In Thee!

82. 狂夜

艾米莉·狄金森

狂夜——狂夜!
与你一起
狂夜一定

忒奢靡！

徒劳——狂风——
于港湾的心——
指南针收起——
海图收起！

泛舟伊甸——
啊，大海！
许我今晚——停泊——
于你！

译后小记

　　此诗是诗人的一首爱情诗。译诗语序和标点与原诗一致，保留原始的节奏和情感不变。

83. *Sand Dunes*

By Robert Frost

Sea waves are green and wet,
But up from where they die,
Rise others vaster yet,
And those are brown and dry.

They are the sea made land
To come at the fisher town,
And bury in solid sand
The men she could not drown.

She may know cove and cape,
But she does not know mankind
If by any change of shape,
She hopes to cut off mind.

Men left her a ship to sink:
They can leave her a hut as well;
And be but more free to think
For the one more cast-off shell.

83. 沙丘

罗伯特·弗罗斯特

海浪潮湿碧绿，
在其消亡之处，
升起更大浪涛，
却是棕黄干燥。

那是海造陆地，
朝向渔村挪移，
欲以黄沙埋葬，
海浪不能溺亡。

熟悉海角海湾，
人类未必了然，
妄想变换形貌，
中断人们思考。

曾经任其沉船，
如今小屋任残；
再扔一枚海贝，
任凭思绪扬飞。

译后小记

罗伯特·弗洛斯特（Robert Frost，1874—1963），美国诗人，曾四度获得普利策奖。

《沙丘》(*Sand Dunes*)全诗四节，描写了他在海滨所见所想。第一节描写海浪潮湿而碧绿，但打到岸上，便顷刻消失不见，正在那时那地，沙丘应运而生，沙丘乃是海浪冲击而成，不过是棕黄干燥。

第二节，诗人继续想象沙丘。诗人把沙丘写成"大海形成的陆地"，因为沙子是被海浪打上岸来的。沙丘会挪移，很可能掩埋沿海的渔村。所以说，没有被海水淹死的人们，但人们很可能被海的另一个形体——沙丘——所吞没。

第三节是诗人进一步的想象。诗人将海拟人化，认为海有感觉有思想，熟悉海角和海湾，却并不能真正了解人类。海的形状在不断地变换，从海浪变成沙丘，但并不能阻止人们的思考和遐想；海浪和沙丘可能会对人类造成危害，但人们会想办法防止这些危害发生。

第四节写诗人看到海浪和沙丘时的遐想。诗人想到大海能翻船，沙丘能掩埋村庄、房屋。想到此处，他往海里扔进了一个海贝，让思绪更自由地飞扬。

全诗四节，每节四行，大多每行六音节，原诗押尾韵，韵式为abab。拙译遵循原诗格律，采用二字顿，以顿代步，每行三顿六字，押尾韵，韵式为aabb。

84. *The Pasture*

By Robert Frost

I'm going out to clean the pasture spring;
I'll only stop to rake the leaves away
(And wait to watch the water clear, I may):
I shan't be gone long. —You come too.

I'm going out to fetch the little calf
That's standing by the mother. It's so young,
It totters when she licks it with her tongue.
I shan't be gone long. —You come too.

84. 牧场

罗伯特·弗罗斯特

我要去清一清牧场泉水；
只消耙去落叶
（也许还等水清澈）；
不会太久——你也来吧！

我要去抱回小牛犊，
站在母牛身边，它太弱小啦，
母牛舌头一舔，它身子便一晃；
不会太久——你也来吧！

译后小记

罗伯特·弗罗斯特(1874—1963)是20世纪最受欢迎的美国诗人之一。他曾当过新英格兰的鞋匠、教师和农场主。他的诗歌从农村生活中汲取题材,与19世纪的诗人有很多共同之处,相比之下,却较少具有现代派气息。他曾赢得4次普利策奖和许多其他的奖励及荣誉,被称为"美国文学中的桂冠诗人"。

《牧场》这首诗是抑扬格五音步诗。清理牧场的流泉,牵回可爱的小牛犊,都是牧场日常工作中再普通不过的事。原诗不难理解,译诗注意语言表达的口吻,字里行间流露的情感,以及整个诗歌语篇的流畅。

85. *Stopping by Woods on a Snowy Evening*

By Robert Frost

Whose woods these are I think I know.
His house is in the village though;
He will not see me stopping here
To watch his woods fill up with snow.

My little horse must think it queer
To stop without a farmhouse near
Between the woods and frozen lake
The darkest evening of the year.

He gives his harness bells a shake
To ask if there is some mistake.
The only other sound's the sweep
Of easy wind and downy flake.

The woods are lovely, dark and deep.
But I have promises to keep,
And miles to go before I sleep,
And miles to go before I sleep.

85. 雪夜林边小驻

罗伯特·弗罗斯特

林子属谁我知晓，
他住村头那条道，
不见我在林边逗，
只为赏雪把路绕。

小马疑惑忙回眸，
前无炊烟却停留，
雪林茫茫湖冻着，
寒夜森森夜里头。

铃儿当当马儿叫，
似问是否迷路了。
林间寂寂无声息，
微风习习雪花飘。

林深幽暗人入迷，
却因诺言不得已，
睡前得走好多里，
睡前得走好多里。

译后小记

诗歌描述了一个冷艳绝美的画面：天色向晚、雪花飘飘、森林幽暗、林中小屋、湖面冰封，诗人驻马赏雪。如此雪景，诗人感叹：虽然偶得这片令人心生退隐之心的美景，但人生前路漫漫，还有遥远的路途要赶，还有许下的种种承诺要履行；人总要履行一生的承诺，才能安心去享受那静谧的良夜美景。

此诗四节，每节四行，每行八音节，抑扬格四音步，行尾押韵（aaba bbcb ccdc dddd），极为流畅自然，音韵节奏感强。

译诗在正确理解原诗语义上译出，步原韵（aaba bbcb ccdc dddd）；以顿代步，一行三顿，有一定的节奏感；保留原诗口语化口吻，特别是最后两句，诗人似乎不舍离开森林美景，口中还在念叨着约定，留下一路远去的背影。

86. *Acquainted with the Night*

By Robert Frost

I have been one acquainted with the night.
I have walked out in rain—and back in rain.
I have outwalked the furthest city light.

I have looked down the saddest city lane.
I have passed by the watchman on his beat
And dropped my eyes, unwilling to explain.

I have stood still and stopped the sound of feet
When far away an interrupted cry
Came over houses from another street,

But not to call me back or say good-bye;
And further still at an unearthly height,
One luminary clock against the sky

Proclaimed the time was neither wrong nor right.
I have been one acquainted with the night.

86. 熟谙黑夜

罗伯特·弗罗斯特

我与黑夜早已熟识,
冒雨出去,冒雨归来,
穿越灯光尽头城市。

阅尽大街小巷悲哀。
擦肩而过看夜守护,
垂下眼帘,不敞胸怀。

蓦然伫立,收敛脚步,
戛然一声,突兀大喊,
穿街越巷,来自远处,

不是唤我,或说再见。
神秘高空,超越尘世,
苍穹之下大钟明现,

彰显时间不是亦是,
我与黑夜早已熟识。

译后小记

这是一首以抑扬格五音步为主旋律的诗,行尾押完全韵 aba bcb cdc ede aa,首尾照应,构成回环,诗歌基调比较压抑。译诗以顿代步,一行八字四顿,行尾步原韵。

有人把此诗的主题解读为"抑郁",其中的"night"就代表"depression",与夜为伍其实就是诗人在描写自己患上抑郁症后与世界相处的感受。也有人认为"night"是主人公在夜晚街道上行走的情景,更体现了现代人的孤独和无家可归之感。诗无达诂,译者最重要的是体验诗人的感受,真实再现情景,而不作过多阐释,具体诗意留待读者解读。

第三节，由于中英语言结构的差异，主句出现在第一行，从句在后两行，而汉语通常不用连接词，按时间先后顺序排列，正常语序是："戛然一声，突兀大喊，穿街越巷，来自远处，（我）蓦然伫立，收敛脚步。"

由于中英语言结构的差异，原诗有很多"I"，译诗除了首尾句重复"我与黑夜早已熟识"，其他转化为无主句。

87. Dust of Snow

By Robert Frost

The way a crow
Shook down on me
The dust of snow
From a hemlock tree

Has given my heart
A change of mood
And saved some part
Of a day I had rued.

87. 雪尘

罗伯特·弗罗斯特

铁杉树上
一只寒鸦
抖动枝丫
雪尘飘扬

他那神态
让我好嗨
心底阴霾
不复存在

译后小记

罗伯特·弗罗斯特的《雪尘》是一首即兴小诗,其短小精悍,一诗两节,每行四个单词(最后一行除外),共三十四个单词,不包含任何形容词,甚至也没有明喻或隐喻,但成功地在读者的内心深处描绘了一幅美丽的图画。第一段写景,第二段抒情,浑若天成,不留琢痕。主旋律为抑扬格二音步,节奏明快,押尾韵 abab cdcd,画面生动,表现了诗人乐观的心态。

译诗按原诗格律,一诗两节,一节四行,每行四字两顿,节奏与原诗一致,行尾有韵脚 abba cccc,力争传递原诗诗意。

88. *Fragmentary Blue*

By Robert Frost

Why make so much of fragmentary blue
In here and there a bird, or butterfly,
Or flower, or wearing-stone, or open eye,
When heaven presents in sheets the solid hue?

Since earth is earth, perhaps, not heaven (as yet)—
Though some savants make earth include the sky;
And blue so far above us comes so high,
It only gives our wish for blue a whet.

88. 蓝色碎片

罗伯特·弗罗斯特

缘何还有如此蓝色碎片
这儿那儿，飞鸟，蝴蝶
鲜花，宝石，明媚的眼
既然天空已然一片蔚蓝？

既然大地是地，(迄今)非天——
虽然学者曾谓天地浑然，
头顶之蓝如此深邃高远，
仅给我们留下蓝色心念。

译后小记

原诗属五音步抑扬格，韵式为抱韵 abba cbbc，译诗紧跟原诗格律，一诗两节，不改变原诗行顺序，以顿代步，一行五顿，营造类似的节奏感，有一定音韵节奏。

89. *Fire and Ice*

By Robert Frost

Some say the world will end in fire,
Some say in ice.
From what I've tasted of desire
I hold with those who favour fire.
But if it had to perish twice,
I think I know enough of hate
To say that for destruction ice
Is also great
And would suffice.

89. 火与冰

罗伯特·弗罗斯特

有人说世界会在火中终结
也有人说世界将被冰毁灭
凭我对于欲望的体验
我赞成火终结说一边
如果世界得毁灭再次
我想仇恨也不分彼此
具有寒冰一样摧毁力
恨若霜剑
不寒而栗

译后小记

这首诗是 20 世纪美国著名的诗人罗伯特·弗罗斯特(Robert Frost, 1874—1963)颇受欢迎的一首抒情诗,作于 1923 年。在诗中,弗罗斯特比较分析了"火"与"冰"这两个极具毁灭性的力量,用火象征激情和欲望,用冰象征冷酷和仇恨。原诗九行,每行八个音节或四个音节,错落有致,形成节奏变化;行尾押韵 abaabcbab。

译诗同样长短不一,押尾韵 aabbcccbc,注意用词的变化,如"终结"与"毁灭",避免重复。原诗题是"火与冰",本想按中文习惯调整为"冰与火",但文中顺序是先写"火",再写"冰",还是按原诗来译吧。

此诗翻译的难点是后五行,按语义层次来理顺。另外,"great"不宜译为"伟大",此处的感情色彩是贬义。

90. The Road Not Taken

By Robert Frost

Two roads diverged in a yellow wood,
And sorry I could not travel both
And be one traveler, long I stood
And looked down one as far as I could
To where it bent in the undergrowth;

Then took the other, as just as fair,
And having perhaps the better claim,
Because it was grassy and wanted wear;
Though as for that the passing there
Had worn them really about the same,

And both that morning equally lay
In leaves no step had trodden black.
Oh, I kept the first for another day!
Yet knowing how way leads on to way,
I doubted if I should ever come back.

I shall be telling this with a sigh
Somewhere ages and ages hence:
Two roads diverged in a wood, and I—
I took the one less traveled by,
And that has made all the difference.

90. 未选择之路

罗伯特·弗罗斯特

黄叶密林，岔出两条小路
惋惜遗恨，无法同时踏足
孤旅独行，良久伫立踟蹰
极目一条，不知延伸何处
弯弯曲曲，蜿蜒林间灌木

选择他途，同样一路芬芳
或许坦诚，风景更好无妨
芳草萋萋，引我欣然前往
设想两途，皆是人来人往
反复踩踏，几乎彼此一样

那日清晨，小路双双静躺
缤纷落叶，无人染足其上
留下其一，期待来日徜徉
路连着路，绵延直至远方
扪心自问，何日旧地重访

年复一年，不知吾身何处
一声叹息，往事遗憾无数
黄叶密林，岔出两条小路
我择其一，一路人烟稀疏
一个抉择，人生由此殊途

译后小记

此诗主旋律为抑扬格四音步,每节的韵式为 abaab,读起来朗朗上口,音韵节奏优美。

全诗共四节,可分两层:一至三节为第一层,在树林里,"我"面临着两条路,而经过思考决定,选择了一条人迹罕至的路。在这一层中,诗人描述了选择人迹罕至的路并不是草率决定的,而是经历了复杂的心理历程。诗人描述了"我"站在岔路口,为不能同时涉足两条路而遗憾,"良久伫立踟蹰",写出"我"的犹豫和久久思索。

"我"终于选择了那条人迹更少的路,就让另一条路留待他日重访,这显然是诗人抉择后的一种自我安慰,因为"路连着路,绵延直至远方/扪心自问,何日旧地重访",虽然如此,但依然义无反顾。

第四节为第二层,是作者多年以后的感慨,"我择其一,一路人烟稀疏/一个抉择,人生由此殊途"。这告诉我们,人的一生面临着无数的选择,而每一次选择都会对人生产生重要影响;一个人的一生怎样度过,就看他在人生的岔路口如何抉择,选择不同,命运就会不同。

译诗以顿代步,每行 10 字 5 顿,每节押韵格式为 aaaaa,希望能再现原诗的音韵节奏与哲学寓意。

91. *Fog*

By Carl Sandburg

The fog comes
On little cat feet.

It sits looking
Over harbor and city
On silent haunches
And then moves on.

91. 雾

卡尔·桑德堡

雾来了
迈着碎猫步。

它蹲坐着
观看城市和港口
静静地
然后重新上路。

译后小记

这是一首意象诗。诗中的雾呈现猫的意象,生动形象,新颖别致。全诗以 cat(猫)为主导,采用了动作意象("The fog comes… It sits looking… and then moves on"),静态意象("on haunches")和听觉意象("silent"),烘托出大雾悄悄弥漫整个城市,而后又悄悄散去的静谧。

92. *The Red Wheelbarrow*

By William Carlos Williams

so much depends

upon

a red wheel

barrow

glazed with rain

water

beside the white

chickens.

92. 红色手推车

威廉·卡洛斯·威廉斯

译文一：

如此之多东西
压着
一辆红色独轮
推车
被雨水淋得
锃亮
旁边还有白色
小鸡

译文二：

如此之多东西堆积在
一地白色小鸡旁
被雨水淋得
锃亮的
一辆
红色
手推
车

译后小记

　　威廉斯的这首短诗是由一个句子构成的自由诗，被推崇为意象派诗歌的名篇。《红色手推车》体现了诗人的一贯主张，即把诗歌创作深深扎根于现实生活中。

　　诗歌所展现的是骤雨初歇时农家院子中的情景，他运用的是静物写生的手法。手推车、雨珠和白鸡都是极为平常的事物，然而，诗人却能以极其细腻的感受能力，通过物体在画面中的特殊定位和鲜明的色彩形成对比，使邻家院子里的雨雾天晴时分那番熟悉景象永恒地被定格在美国文学史上。整首诗读来清新自然，色彩鲜明，动静结合，情景堪画。在诗歌的形式上，诗人也颇具有独创。他似乎认为在描述这些平凡的事物时无须采用大写字母，因此，全诗所有单词均采用小写形式。

　　译文一紧贴原诗形式，译文二将句子语序自然调整，诗文的形状是否看起来像一辆堆满东西的独轮车呢？诗无达诂，译无定法，于是如此译之。

93. *Ars Poetica*

By Archibald Macleish

A poem should be palpable and mute
As a globed fruit,

Dumb
As old medallions to the thumb,

Silent as the sleeve-worn stone
Of casement ledges where the moss has grown—

A poem should be wordless
As the flight of birds.

*

A poem should be motionless in time
As the moon climbs,

Leaving, as the moon releases
Twig by twig the night-entangled trees,

Leaving, as the moon behind the winter leaves,
Memory by memory the mind—

A poem should be motionless in time
As the moon climbs.

<pre>
                          *
A poem should be equal to:
Not true.

For all the history of grief
An empty doorway and a maple leaf.

For love
                          *
The leaning grasses and two lights above the sea—

A poem should not mean
But be.
</pre>

93. 诗艺

阿奇博尔德·麦克利什

诗应静默而可感知
如滚圆果子

不语
如旧奖章之于拇指

不言如衣袖磨平
的窗台石,青苔悄生——

无声
如鸟翱翔
　　　　　*

诗应静驻时光
任月攀升

隽永，任月一枝一枝
解开被黑夜纠缠的树

隽永，任月在冬身后离去
记忆于心田——

诗应静驻时光
任月攀升
　　　　　*
诗不应
写实

人生寂寥
化作"空阶枫叶飘"

爱意缠绵
化作芳草依依光数——
诗者，不言
而是也

译后小记

阿齐博尔德·麦克利什（Archibald Macleish）于1892年出生在美国，《诗艺》是诗人麦克利什对于"诗歌当为艺术论"的诗，其语言表达也颇有诗意，翻译的理解和表达都有相当难度。这首诗有三部分，每部分有四个两行诗节。诗人解读了什么是"诗艺"，诗者可意会不可言传也。从语篇连贯来看，原诗"A poem should be … mute … Dumb…Silent…A poem should be wordless …A poem should be motionless …A poem should not mean but be"，拙译"诗应静默……不语……不言……诗应无声……诗应静驻……诗者，不言/而是也"对应译出。

第一部分，诗人用了四个比喻来表达何为诗，理解不易，表达更难，表达需要炼字才能出诗意。

第二部分，主要脉络为"A poem should be motionless…Leaving…Leaving … Memory by memory the mind— A poem should be motionless…"这里的"leave"究竟为何意，"离开"还是"留下"？译者们对于"Leaving… Memory by memory the mind"的理解分歧比较大，常见自相矛盾的翻译，如"诗应静驻时光，如月攀升"之类。主要原因有二，一是因为"leaving"字面上本可以表示一对反义词"留下"与"离开"，二是跨行诗句，分析起来不容易。

Halliday 和 Hasan 认为词汇衔接（复现与同现）是语篇连贯的重要手段。词汇衔接指通过词的重复、同义、反义、上下义、互补、同现等词汇间的语义关系来实现语篇连贯。在同一语篇中，围绕着某个话题，相关的词汇往往同时出现。Ars Poetica 一诗中，"motionless"（静止不动）与"leaving"一起描写"诗"，"leaving"与"motionless"是异词同义复现关系，语义应该一致，故"leaving"也应该是"静止""不动""留下"之意。

这里"motionless"与"climb""release""leave"构成一静三动对比，正是反义同现关系。"诗静驻时光"与"月的攀升"形成对比，那么后面的"leaving"就不难理解了；任凭月亮走了，"诗应静驻时光"，那就应该是"留下记忆"。"Leaving … Memory by memory the mind"实为"Leaving…the mind memory by memory"的倒装。

第二小节的句子可以整理成这么一句话，分为主句与四个状语从句："A poem should be motionless in time … Leaving … Leaving … Memory by memory the mind—A poem should be motionless in time"（诗应静驻时光……隽永……隽永……记忆于心田——诗应静驻时光……）为主句，中间的省略号是四个插入语"As the moon climbs""As the moon releases twig by twig the night-entangled trees""As the moon behind the winter leaves""As the moon climbs"（任月攀升，任月一枝一枝解开被黑夜纠缠的树，任月在冬身后离去，任月一枝一枝解开被黑夜纠缠的树）。

第三部分的第一节："A poem should be equal to: not true"。诗人主张"诗不应写实话"，如果要写哀愁，就不应该在诗里写"哀愁"，而是应该写"空阶枫叶落"，如果要写爱情，就不应该在诗里写"爱情"，而是应该写"芳草依依数点光"。日本人夏目漱石也说，"我爱你"，不能说"我爱你"，而应该说"今夜月色真美"。"哀愁""我爱你"都是毫无诗意的大实话，不应这么写进诗歌。

第三部分的第四节，"A poem should not mean/but be"呼应第一节"A poem should be … mute … Dumb…Silent…wordless"，跟前面也呼应，诗应静默、不言、不语、无声。诗应该意会，不可言传，故最后一节译为"诗者，不言/而是也"。

94. Dreams

By James Langston Hughes

Hold fast to dreams
For if dreams die
Life is a broken-winged bird
That cannot fly.

Hold fast to dreams
For when dreams go
Life is a barren field
Frozen with snow.

94. 梦想

詹姆斯·兰斯顿·休斯

紧紧抓住梦想
因为梦想失去
如同小鸟断翅
生活了无生趣

赶紧抓住梦想
因为梦想离开
生活如同荒原
冰雪霜冻掩埋

译后小记

詹姆斯·兰斯顿·休斯（James Langston Hughes 1902—1967）是美国著名的黑人诗人、作家。

"dreams"代表美好的希望和理想，也代表着饱受歧视的美国黑人对自由、平等和民权的向往，是黑人在忍受压迫、剥削和社会各种不公待遇时的精神支柱，契合1960年黑人领袖马丁·路德·金在《我有一个梦想》（*I Have a Dream*）中所表达的思想。此诗短小精悍，立意直接，用词简单，节奏明快，朗朗上口。

"Hold fast"，包含两层语义，"赶紧抓住"和"紧紧抓住"，故一、二小节第一行"Hold fast to dreams"在翻译时结合下文诗句，各取一个视角，选择不同表达。

95. Do Not Stand at My Grave and Weep

By Mary Elizabeth Frye

Do not stand at my grave and weep,
I am not there, I do not sleep.
I am a thousand winds that blow.
I am the diamond glints on snow.
I am the sunlight on ripened grain.
I am the gentle autumn's rain.
When you awaken in the morning's hush,
I am the swift uplifting rush
Of quiet birds in circled flight.
I am the soft stars that shine at night.
Do not stand at my grave and cry;
I am not there, I did not die.

95. 不要悲伤我墓前

玛丽·伊丽莎白·弗莱伊

不要悲伤我墓前
我未在此永长眠
我乃清风空中游
我乃白雪晶莹透
我乃阳光照万物

我乃秋雨任倾诉

清晨静谧中醒来

我是那振翅翱翔

盘旋空中的飞鸟

我是闪烁的星星

不要哭泣我墓前

我未在此永长眠

译后小记

据说这是弗莱伊在1932年为她的一位德籍犹太裔朋友玛格利特·舒瓦兹·科普夫写的一首诗。玛格利特此前一直在担心她远在德国生病的母亲，而愈演愈烈的反犹太运动使她难以与母亲团聚，当她得知母亲去世的消息后，她告诉玛丽·弗莱伊她无法到母亲墓前悲悼了。

弗莱伊写了这首诗，作为对逝者的吊唁。

原诗12行，每行基本为8个音节，抑扬格四音步，行尾押韵aabbccddee，非常工整。

96. *Oil That Glitters*

By Felicia Lamport

The sudden renewal

Of access to fuel

Sheds this instructive light:

The end of a crisis

Occurs when the price is

Jacked to the proper height.

96. 闪光的石油

费利西娅·兰波特

闪光的石油

突然不再限流

不再供不应求

世界恍然大悟

价格升至适当高度

能源危机随之结束

译后小记

20 世纪 70 年代初期和中期，石油输出国组织（OPEC）为了抬高油价，几次限制石油的生产和输出，在西方世界引起能源危机。美国诗人和讽刺作家费利西娅·兰波特（1916—1999）写的这首诗——*Oil That Glitters*，说的就是这件事。这首诗发表在 1976 年 12 月号的《大西洋月刊》（*The Atlantic*，December，1976）。

这首小诗，格律比较严谨："renewal"和"fuel"构成双韵，"crisis"和"price is"（连读）押的也可算是马赛克韵，"light"和"height"是一对单韵；原诗韵式是 aabccb（一对联韵 aa 加上四行抱韵 bccb），译诗采用尾韵 aaabbb。

97. Parting

By Wu Ningkun

Finally you are gone

Leaving behind a quiet autumn

And fallen leaves all over the ground

A light breeze will blow it all away

Duckweeds of memory

Sighs of fallen flowers

Notes of vows and pledges

Tears of pearls

And I free as a floating cloud

A light breeze will blow it all away

Sparkling of morn dew

Wistfulness of the setting sun

Mists of life

Last night's dream

And my heart still as still water

And the water like a mirror

And who can the young face

Be languishing for

97. 分别

巫宁坤

终究　你走了
落下　一秋的寂寥
落下　满地的黄叶

一阵微风　将一切吹散
记忆的浮萍
落花的长叹
声声的誓言
珠也似的泪
而我　漂浮如云

一阵微风　将一切吹散
晨露的晶莹
夕阳的惆怅
人生的迷雾
昨夜的遗梦
而我　心如止水

那水　若明镜
照见　为谁朱颜瘦
照见　为谁人憔悴

译后小记

巫宁坤(1920—2019),男,江苏扬州人。中国著名翻译家,英美文学研究专家。

这是一首别离忧伤之歌,却依旧唯美,翻译时,原诗中淡淡的忧伤,化作每一个字符,节奏、语气、措辞依旧是翻译的关键点。

译诗四节,第一节与第四节,每节三行,结构类似,字数相当,每行中间有一停顿,因为"你"的离开,每一次都会撕裂"我"的心,不可能语气流畅明快,译者在此处的停顿出于自己的体验感。在第一节和第四节,运用了反复,重复了"落下""照见",更符合"我"怀念"你"的心底节奏。

第二节与第三节采用同样的结构,"你"的离去,如同"一阵微风,将一切吹散",诗人历数"我"对"你"的怀念。

译诗是对原诗的阐释,不知对于此诗结构的微调是否更好地表达了原诗的情感?许渊冲先生说"文学翻译是两种语言的竞赛",在翻译这首诗时,译者感受深刻。

98. A Farewell

By Robert Burns

Go fetch to me a pint o'wine,
  An'fill it in a silver tassie;
That I may drink before I go
  A service to my bonnie lassie:
The boat rocks at the pier o'Leith,
  Fu' loud the wind blaws frae the Ferry,
The ship rides by the Berwick-law,
  And I maun leave my bonnie Mary.

The trumpets sound, the banners fly,
  The glittering spears are ranked ready;
The shouts o' war are heard afar,
  The battle closes thick and bloody;
But it's not the roar o' sea or shore
  Wad make me langer wish to tarry;
Nor shouts o'war that's heard afar—
  It's leaving thee, my bonnie Mary.

98. 告别

罗伯特·彭斯

请来一品脱美酒,
  斟满银色的酒杯；

临行干杯再开走，
　　　敬我漂亮的宝贝：
船在利斯港颠簸，
　　　劲风吹拂着渡口，
船沿圆顶山驶离，
　　　我得告别好玛丽。

号角声声旗帜扬，
　　　长矛齐备闪闪亮；
硝烟袅袅厮杀声，
　　　战斗激烈而血腥；
不是大海的咆哮
　　　让我渴望多逗留；
也非战争的喧嚣——
　　　是要远离我甜妞。

译后小记

　　这首诗歌最为特别之处在于，世间最为温柔的爱情与最为惨烈的战争并置，这边是小船野渡，美酒佳人，窃窃私语，缠绵悱恻；那边是刀枪雨林，旌旗飘舞，鼓角峥嵘，呐喊震天。诗中多苏格兰方言，所以此诗比较难理解。

　　原诗共两节，每节前四行为抑扬格四音步，后四行节奏发生变化，反映诗人即将离开时难以平复的心情。译诗理清原诗思路，尽量做到语义连贯，情感一致。

99. *My Heart's in the Highlands*

By Robert Burns

My heart's in the highlands, my heart is not here;
My heart's in the highlands a-chasing the deer;
Chasing the wild deer, and following the roe,
My heart's in the highlands wherever I go.

Farewell to the highlands, farewell to the North,
The birth-place of valor, the country of worth;
Wherever I wander, wherever I rove,
The hills of the highlands for ever I love.

Farewell to the mountains high cover'd with snow;
Farewell to the straths and green valleys below;
Farewell to the forests and wild-hanging woods;
Farewell to the torrents and loud-pouring floods.

My heart's in the highlands, my heart is not here;
My heart's in the highlands a-chasing the deer;
Chasing the wild deer, and following the roe,
My heart's in the highlands wherever I go.

99. 我心在苏格兰高地

罗伯特·彭斯

我的心呀在高地,不在这里;
我心追逐群鹿在高地;
追逐着那野鹿,追逐着那獐鹿,
我心在高地,无论身居何处。

告别高地,告别北方,
勇士的家乡,无价的故土;
无论我漫步何方,无论我漫游何处,
永远爱恋着那高地山冈。

再见,白雪皑皑的高高山峦;
再见,青翠欲滴的河谷溪川;
再见,莽莽野生的森林树丛;
再见,咆哮激流的奔腾汹涌。

我的心呀在高地,不在这里;
我心追逐群鹿在高地;
追逐着那野鹿,追逐着那獐鹿,
我心在高地,无论身居何处。

译后小记

诗题"My Heart's in the Highlands"一般译为"我心在高原",考虑受众为中文读者,笔者译为"我心在苏格兰高地"。

诗人彭斯的感情豪迈而奔放。他大声呼喊:"我的心,在高地!"苏格兰高地不仅是一个地理位置上的故乡,更是心灵的家园,精神的栖息地。全诗每行11个音节左右,采用aabb韵式,反复咏唱,前后呼应,极富节奏感和感染力。

译诗在语义内在连贯和情感与原诗保持一致的基础上,追求音韵节奏之美。

100. *We Real Cool*

By Gwebdolyn Brooks

The Pool Players. Seven at the Golden Shovel.

We real cool. We
Left school. We

Lurk late. We
Strike straight. We

Sing sin. We
Thin gin. We

Jazz June. We
Die soon.

100. 我们真酷

格温多林·布鲁克斯

台球玩家。七点在金铲子酒吧。

我们真酷。我们
逃学不读。我们

彻夜在外。我们
球技不赖。我们

饮酒作乐。我们
纵情声色。我们

跳舞搞怪。我们
归天快哉。

译后小记

此诗短小精悍，每一句只有3个单词，字字精辟。这首跨行、跨节诗，诗人使用语法变异、排列变异、书写变异等手法，通过反讽的方式，来劝诫当时的年轻黑人学生们莫虚度光阴，莫浪费美好人生。

根据上下文语境，"We left school"译成"逃学"更符合诗意；"We lurk late"译成"夜不归宿，彻夜游荡"；"We strike straight"指球技高超，一杆进洞；"We sing sin"形容当时的年轻人不以作恶为耻，反以为荣；"We thin gin"指年轻人畅饮兑水的劣质杜松子酒，不思进取；"We jazz june"指年轻人在酒吧纵情歌舞；最后一句"We die soon"用来警醒众人。

参考文献

[1] Beaugrande R de, Dressler W. Introduction to text linguistics[M]. London & New York: Longman, 1981: 3-13.

[2] Catford J C. A linguistic theory of translation [M]. Oxford: Oxford University Press, 1965.

[3] Christiane Nord. Translating as a purposeful activity-functionalist approaches explained [M]. Shanghai: Shanghai Foreign Language Education Press, 2001.

[4] Fussel Paul. Poetic meter and poetic form[M]. New York: Random House, 1965.

[5] Jakobson R. What is poetry? [M] // Jakobson R. Language in literature. Massachusetts and London: The Belknap Press of Harvard University Press, 1987: 368-378.

[6] Halliday M A K, Hasan R. Cohesion in English [M]. Shanghai: Foreign Language and Research Press, 2001.

[7] McAuley J. *Versification*: a short introduction[M]. East Lansing: Michigan State University Press, 1966.

[8] Papegaaij B, Schubert K. Text coherence in translation [M]. Dordrecht: Foris Publication, 1988.

[9] Shklovsky V. Art as technique[C]//David Lodge. Modern criticism and theory: a reader. London: Longman, 1988: 20.

[10] Todorov T. The poetics of prose[M]. Ithaca, New York: Cornell University Press, 1977.

[11] Todorov T. Introduction to poetics[M]. Minneapolis: University of

Minnesota Press，1981.

[12] 卞之琳. 英国诗选[M]. 北京：商务印书馆，1996.

[13] 陈刚. 西湖诗赞[M]. 杭州：浙江摄影出版社，1996.

[14] 陈宏薇. 汉英翻译基础[M]. 上海：上海外语教育出版社，1998.

[15] 陈君朴. 汉英对照唐诗绝句150首[M]. 上海：上海大学出版社，2005.

[16] 丰华瞻. 丰华瞻译诗集[M]. 上海：上海外语教育出版社，1997.

[17] 冯庆华. 红译艺坛[M]. 上海：上海外语教育出版社，2006.

[18] 搞口译的也可以留芳[EB/OL]. [2007-05-02]. http://www.tianya.cn/publicforum/content/english/1/117292.shtml.

[19] Milkias Mehreteab Yohannes. It is better to die *a thousand times than live without dignity*[EB/OL]. [2011-01-23]. http://awate.com/category/articles.

[20] 辜正坤，译注. 毛泽东诗词：英汉对照韵译[M]. 北京：北京大学出版社，1993.

[21] 顾正阳. 古诗词曲英译美学研究[M]. 上海：上海大学出版社，2006.

[22] 郭建中. 当代美国翻译理论[M]. 武汉：湖北教育出版社，2000.

[23] 黄杲炘. 英诗汉译学[M]. 上海：上海外语教育出版社，2007.

[24] 黄杲炘，译. 柔巴依一百首[M]. 北京：中国对外翻译出版公司，1998.

[25] 江枫. 论文学翻译及汉语汉字[M]. 北京：华文出版社，2009.

[26] 李云启. 英诗赏读与美感再植[M]. 北京：人民出版社，2007.

[27] 刘坤尊. 英诗的音韵格律[M]. 桂林：广西师范大学出版社，2011.

[28] 罗良功. 英诗概论[M]. 武汉：武汉大学出版社，2002.

[29] 罗义蕴，曹明伦，陈朴. 英诗金库[M]. 成都：四川人民出版社，

1987.

[30] 毛荣贵. 新世纪大学英汉翻译教程[M]. 上海：上海交通大学出版社，2002.

[31] 毛泽东. 纪念白求恩[M]. 北京：东方红出版社，1967.

[32] 穆诗雄. 诗歌鉴赏的差异性与诗歌翻译[J]. 外语与外语教学，2005(2)：33-36.

[33] 聂珍钊. 英语诗歌形式导论[M]. 北京：中国社会科学出版社，2007.

[34] 潘文国. "语文歧视"会引发汉语危机吗[N]. 解放日报，2011-2-7（5）.

[35] 蒲度戎. 押韵诗歌欣赏[M]. 重庆：重庆大学出版社，2008.

[36] 齐晓燕. 英诗的美学探究[M]. 北京：中国传媒大学出版社，2008.

[37] 沈苏儒. 翻译的最高境界"信达雅"漫谈[M]. 北京：中国对外翻译出版公司，2006.

[38] 施仲谋，等. 中华文化承传（上册）[M]. 北京：北京大学出版社，2007.

[39] 石璞. 英诗初阶[M]. 西安：西北工业大学出版社，1987.

[40] 宋天锡. 翻译新概念：英汉互译实用教程[M]. 北京：国防工业出版社，2007.

[41] 唐一鹤，注译. 英译唐诗三百首[M]. 天津：天津人民出版社，2005.

[42] 涂宗涛. 诗词曲格律纲要[M]. 天津：天津人民出版社，2000.

[43] 《毛泽东诗词》翻译组. 毛泽东诗词[M]. 北京：外文出版社，1999.

[44] 汪榕培. 英译陶诗[M]. 北京：商务印书馆，1996.

[45] 王大濂. 英译唐诗绝句百首[M]. 天津：百花文艺出版社，1997.

［46］王东风. 诗意与诗意的翻译[J]. 外语研究，2018(1)：56-64.

［47］王东风. 小说翻译的语义连贯重构[J]. 中国翻译，2005(3)：37-43.

［48］王东风. 连贯与翻译[M]. 上海：上海外语教育出版社，2009.

［49］王雪松. 论标点符号与中国现代诗歌节奏的关系[J]. 中国现代文学研究丛刊，2016(3)：158-174.

［50］王永泰. 旅游广告及俗语外译的艺术美［J］. 上海翻译，2007（1）.

［51］吴伟雄，吴庆雯. 新编英汉翻译速通[M]. 武汉：武汉大学出版社，2009.

［52］吴伟雄. 好易学英汉笔译[M]. 广州：世界图书出版公司，2000.

［53］吴伟雄. 谈涉外活动中诗词佳句汉英翻译的现场效果[J]. 上海科技翻译，2004(1)：28-31.

［54］吴翔林. 英语格律诗及自由诗［M］. 北京：商务印书馆，1993.

［55］谢天振. 当代国外翻译理论导读[M]. 天津：南开大学出版社，2008.

［56］许渊冲. 翻译的标准[J]. 翻译通讯，1981(1)：1.

［57］许渊冲. 翻译的艺术[M]. 北京：五洲传播出版社，2006.

［58］许渊冲. 汉英对照唐诗三百首[M]. 北京：高等教育出版社，2000.

［59］许渊冲. 文学与翻译[M]. 北京：北京大学出版社，2003.

［60］许渊冲. 英汉对照唐诗三百首［M］. 北京：高等教育出版社，2001.

［61］许渊冲. 中诗英韵探胜[M]. 北京：北京大学出版社，1992.

［62］许渊冲. 山阴道上[M]. 北京：中央编译出版社，2005.

［63］许渊冲. 诗书人生[M]. 天津：百花文艺出版社，2003：96.

［64］许渊冲. 文学与翻译[M]. 北京：北京大学出版社，2003.

[65] 许渊冲,等.唐诗三百首新译[M].北京:中国对外翻译出版公司,1998.

[66] 许渊冲,译.楚辞[M].长沙:湖南出版社,1994.

[67] 许渊冲,译.毛泽东诗词选[M].北京:中国对外翻译出版公司,1993.

[68] 许渊冲.汉英对照宋词三百首[M].北京:高等教育出版社,2004.

[69] 许渊冲.唐诗三百首:汉英对照(2版).北京:五洲传播出版社,2018.

[70] 杨宪益,戴乃迭.楚辞选[M].北京:外文出版社,2001.

[71] 臧克家.毛泽东诗词鉴赏[M].郑州:河南文艺出版社,2005.

[72] 张美芳.翻译研究的功能途径[M].上海:上海外语教育出版社,2005.

[73] 张智中.汉诗英译的标点之美[J].井冈山大学学报(社会科学版),2015(2):100-105.

[74] 张智中.汉诗英译美学研究[M].北京:商务印书馆,2015.

[75] 郑鉴枢.楹联讲座[M].深圳:海天出版社,1993.

[76] 周领顺.英译汉之"好":好在哪里?[J].西安外国语大学学报,2018(4).

[77] 周领顺.从文化解读到语言定位[J].中国翻译,2018(6):108-111.

[78] 周仪,罗平.翻译与批评[M].武汉:湖北教育出版社,1999.

[79] 追求"信、达、雅"杨宪益获翻译文化终身成就奖[EB/OL].[2009-09-17].http://www.china.com.cn/culture/txt/2009-09/17/content_18547077.htm.